Christmas Unwrapped

ROSE MALONE

©**Copyright 2023 by Rose Malone - All rights reserved.**

In no way is it legal to reproduce, duplicate, or transmit any part of this document in either electronic means or in printed format. Recording of this publication is strictly prohibited, and any storage of this document is not allowed unless with written permission from the publisher.

All rights reserved.

Respective authors own all copyrights not held by the publisher.

TABLE OF CONTENTS

Chapter 1 1
Chapter 2 19
Chapter 3 38
Chapter 4 54
Chapter 5 73
Chapter 6 88
Chapter 7 107
Chapter 8 131
Chapter 9 145
Chapter 10 163
Chapter 11 179
Chapter 12 196
Bonus Recipe 200
About The Author 204

INTRODUCTION

Snowflakes are falling, carols are ringing, the folks of Edgartown are getting robbed blind, and worse, some kids may be in big trouble...

Mary Hogan is really looking forward to the Annual Christmas in Edgartown Weekend to kick off the Holiday Season, that is until a string of unusual events start to occur around her and her friends. There is a pickpocket on the loose, someone attempts to break into her best friend's mansion, and there's a strange new neighbor lurking around. Where's a large cup of eggnog when you need one?

But Mary, with the help of her friends, her psychic abilities, and her trusty pets, is not going to let some nefarious characters ruin their holiday cheer. But it might take more than her investigation skills to solve these crimes.

It might just take a Christmas miracle...

CHAPTER 1

"I hate Christmas."

Mary turned from studying the twelve-foot tree that the delivery men from the tree farm had just set up in its stand. The giant blue spruce seemed to be leaning just a tad to the left. But probably now was not the time to mention that slight issue.

She frowned at her friend. "Sharon, that's not true. You love Christmas."

"At my house, yes." Sharon tugged a dust sheet from another piece of furniture, revealing a stunning Chippendale settee. "Not in this moldering old place."

Mary glanced around at the stunning Edgartown historic mansion. Moldering was definitely not the word she would use to describe it. Opulent, yes. Lavish, yes. Stunning, definitely. But moldering. No way!

But she didn't say that, instead giving her friend a caring look.

Mary knew Sharon's choice of description was her friend's way of coping with the painful emotions that being back in the mansion stirred up. Mary had no idea how long it had been since Sharon set foot in the place.

The Peabody Mansion was a breathtaking historic home. One of the gems of North Water Street, Edgartown. Sharon had been left the mansion by her husband—her third husband to be exact. He passed away maybe close to four years ago now. Mary always suspected that Edwin James Peabody III had been Sharon's only true love.

Edwin was twenty years older than Sharon, but their age difference hadn't mattered. The two of them had just understood and adored each other. Unfortunately, their marriage had only lasted a few years due to Edwin's health issues. He'd had a bad heart, which had left Sharon with a broken one when he passed. Mary knew that was why Sharon hadn't parted with the gorgeous old mansion. But it was also why Sharon didn't want to live here. Too many memories.

"Why did you agree to participate in the Edgartown's Christmas house tour?" Mary asked, gently. "This is already such a busy time of year. Getting ready for this tour and dealing with all the tourists here for the weekend really is just an added stress."

Mary had always loved the tradition of the annual Christmas in Edgartown weekend. She loved the holiday parade, the lighting of the Harbor Lighthouse, and the Victorian Christmas Carolers who invited all of the public to join them for the celebration and caroling on the magnificent wrap-around porch of the historic Harborside Inn built in the 1890's.

But out of all the weekend festivities, Mary's favorite was the Historic Home Holiday Tour. Where homeowners allowed guests in to see their gorgeous homes and all their exquisite decorations. Being inside these homes that had once belonged to sea captains and people who made their fortunes from whaling and shipping was like walking back in time. All that grandeur and old money.

But preparing for the tour was a lot of work, and hosting hoards of strangers in your home could be pretty darned invasive.

"Because Edwin loved it. He got such a kick out of it" Sharon replied as she collapsed on the settee with a sigh. "And I've finally accepted that I need to come to a decision about this place. I was recently contacted by a realtor with a really good offer. A couple from New York want to buy the place, contents and all, for a bed-and-breakfast. Sorry, I know, more potential competition for The Emerald Inn. "Mary shook her head dismissively. "I'm not worried about that, Edgartown attracts a different kind of guest than West Tisbury. But, more importantly, are you sure you want to sell?"

Sharon shrugged, then nodded. "Yes, it's time. I'll never move back here. But Edwin would want me to show the place one last time before I sell it. And truthfully, I want to do it for him. But holy mackerel, it's a lot of work." Then she pointed a finger at Mary and added, "I refuse to dress up as Santa, though."

Mary laughed, suddenly recalling Edwin in his Santa suit. "Edwin did dress up as Santa, didn't he?"

"Every blasted year," Sharon groaned. Mary caught her friend's fond smile as she dropped her head back against the sofa.

Could Sharon really sell all this? There were just as many wonderful memories here as there were sad ones.

"I'm glad you hired a crew to come help you decorate tomorrow. That will make things a lot easier."

Sharon lifted her head and smiled halfheartedly. "It will. But I still have to be here to direct everything."

Mary knew that would be stressful for her friend, too. There was a lot of work to be done in a very short time.

"Plus, I don't want to deal with the Gossip Gang," Sharon added, rolling her eyes. "Heaven knows, they'll show up for the tour just to have a running commentary about every garland and every ornament. And of course, how I married Edwin for his money."

Mary frowned with annoyance. Talk about old news on that particular piece of gossip. Sharon was right, however. There was a group of women in this town that lived to do nothing else but talk about every living soul within a 30-mile radius, maybe even more!

She glanced around the living room. Most of the sheets that protected the furniture had been removed, and the place already looked like a million bucks, even without all of the Christmas ornamentation.

Several million bucks, Mary suspected.

Built in 1823, all of the rooms of the Peabody Mansion had fourteen-foot ceilings trimmed with ornate crown molding. The living room was decorated in warm burgundies and rich golds with silk curtains and large windows that overlooked the front porch and North Water Street. Perfectly preserved antiques showcased the wealth and opulence of years gone by. It was hard to imagine the Gossip Gang could find anything to criticize about the historic mansion's decor. Yet Mary knew they would.

"I think it's time for happy hour," Sharon stated, then pushed herself up from the sofa. "Martini anyone?"

Mary smiled. "I'll have a small one."

She wasn't a huge fan of Sharon's favorite cocktail, but she didn't think Sharon should be drinking alone.

Sharon headed through the many rooms toward the kitchen at the back of the house, only to pause, looking out a window in the dining room.

"That's odd. There's someone at the house next door. The Vanderhoops never come to the Vineyard in the winter. They are part of the summer crowd."

Mary joined Sharon at the window. Sure enough, there were two people going around the side of the equally beautiful home next door and heading toward a bulkhead that led to the house's cellar.

"Maybe they're workmen or something."

Mary, on the other hand, wasn't sure that referring to them as workmen was accurate. They were so bundled up it was hard to determine even what gender they were. Mary was fairly certain the one with the torn jacket and dirty jeans was probably male, but the second one who was thin and short and swimming in a stained puffer coat, made it harder to tell if this was a male or female.

Sharon frowned. "They must be workmen. They certainly don't look like any of the Vanderhoop clan. None of that family would be caught dead in dirty jeans and a ripped parka," she said with a laugh. "Not even to do handiwork. Casual attire for that family is Ralph Lauren and Lacoste all the way."

From Sharon's tone Mary got the feeling she wasn't a big fan of the Vanderhoops. And as she watched the two people opening the bulkhead, Mary's head started to hum. She liked to call this familiar buzz her intuition, although she knew it was something a bit more than that.

The situation didn't feel quite right. And it wasn't just their lack of designer clothing. Who were they? And what were they doing?

"Maybe we should call the police. Just to be safe," Mary suggested.

Sharon shrugged. "Well, they're going into the basement, so they probably are workmen. Maybe there's an emergency with the plumbing or heating. I'm sure it's nothing strange. The Vanderhoops have that house locked down like a vault, so it must be okay for them to be there. But I'll keep an eye on the place anyway."

Sharon continued to the kitchen. Mary remained at the window, watching. Maybe she should go over and introduce herself just to get a better feel for what they were doing here.

Nope, none of my business, she told herself adamantly. It was Christmastime, and she wasn't going to get herself involved in more amateur sleuthing. If Sharon didn't think it was a big deal then she would go with that. Mary had done more than enough investigating over the past few months as it was. Plus, if those guys were up to something suspicious, they surely wouldn't be wandering around the Vanderhoops property in broad daylight.

Okay, it was closer to dusk, but still, anyone could see them roaming around the mansion. That wasn't the behavior of criminals, and she knew criminals from her days as a lawyer.

And from her days as a caterer for that matter.

Mary stayed at the window until the two had disappeared down the steps into the cellar, then she followed Sharon into the kitchen.

Her friend stood at the marble kitchen island, expertly mixing two martinis. Once they were properly shaken and poured into martini glasses, the women both sat down at the island.

"To Edwin," Sharon said with a bittersweet smile as she raised her drink.

"To Edwin," Mary echoed, and they clinked their glasses together.

Mary took a sip. The martini was stronger than her usual glass of wine, but she hoped the hard liquor would calm the buzzing in her brain.

"So, I'll plan to be over here by noon to help you with the decorating crew," Mary offered, determined to focus on the tasks at hand. "And then we can head over to the lighthouse for the lighting ceremony."

"Perfect," Sharon agreed.

The lighting of the Edgartown Harbor Lighthouse was one of Mary's favorite Christmas traditions. When she and her father would come to visit Aunt Bridget for the holidays, they would never miss the lighting ceremony.

Mary had hoped that her father would be able to make it up from Florida to join her this year, but her dad was participating in the Christmas Classic, a golfing tournament that his retirement community was hosting this year.

Dad loved his golf. And Mary couldn't begrudge him living his best retired life. Plus, he would be here for Christmas Day proper, and even staying until after New Year's.

Besides, going to the lighting ceremony with Sharon was the next best thing anyway. Sharon had been her Aunt Bridget's best friend, and in many ways, Mary considered Sharon almost like an aunt, too.

Mary took one more sip of the martini and then set it down. "Is there anything you wanted to work on this evening?"

Sharon polished off her martini, then shook her head. "Tomorrow is going to be a busy day. I think I'll just lock up the place for the night and head home to get some rest."

Her usually unstoppable friend did look tired tonight. This was a lot of emotion for Sharon to deal with, and especially at this time of year.

"I need to head home, too. I'm sure Starlight is getting desperate for her evening walk."

Mary could swear that her beloved German Shepherd's sense of time was better than Greenwich Mean Time, and she knew her dog would be waiting at the front door for her, wondering what the delay was on their walk schedule. "I'm also going to do a test run on my entry for the Christmas baking competition. I'm winning that darned thing this year, even if it kills me!"

"What are you entering?"

"Aunt Bridget's pumpkin bread."

Sharon groaned. "Oh Lord, that bread. I swear I'm still carrying around five extra pounds from that bread. But it's worth it. That stuff is so delicious."

Mary grinned. She had to agree. The recipe was definitely worth every extra calorie.

With their plans in place, both women stood. But before they could gather up their coats and get ready to leave there was a knock at the door.

"Who could that be?" Sharon blurted out, surprised.

She headed to answer it. Mary followed.

When Sharon opened the large, mahogany front door, they were both surprised to see a young man with slicked back hair and clad totally in dark blue.

"Good evening, ladies. I'm an officer with the Edgartown Police." With a serious expression, and a slight nod of his head, he flashed a badge. "I'm sorry to interrupt your evening, but we're going around town to let the residents know that there have been a few break-ins in the area over the past week. We just want to make the residents aware and remind you to make sure your homes are locked up. And to set your alarm systems, if you have one."

"That's awful," Sharon said. "But thank you for letting us know. And yes, I do have an alarm system, so I'll be sure to set it when I leave."

The officer nodded with approval. "That's good. I know this house is usually vacant, isn't it? Are you staying here for the holidays?"

"No, I'm getting the house ready for the Christmas house tour. But I'm not staying here at night."

The officer smiled again. "Well, we aren't trying to scare anyone, but we do want people to be cautious. I'm sure we'll capture the culprits soon."

Although he sounded confident, a shiver prickled down Mary's spine.

As the officer turned to leave, Mary couldn't help but ask, "Do you have any suspects yet?"

The officer turned back, shaking his head. "No, not yet. So, just be vigilant."

Mary immediately thought of the two strangers that she and Sharon had seen earlier. Could they be the culprits? She didn't want to jump to any conclusions, but the humming in her head was back.

"Have you been to the house next-door yet?" Mary asked, gesturing in the direction of the Vanderhoop's house.

The officer frowned, then said, "Yes, I spoke to them just before I came over here."

Because his tone suggested he hadn't found the people suspicious, Mary decided she was probably overthinking the situation.

After the policeman had moved back down the sidewalk, Sharon asked, "Are you getting a strange feeling about those guys at the Vanderhoops?"

Mary turned towards Sharon, probably a little too quickly. "I just figured it would be good to ask. The officer doesn't seem concerned about them, so I'm sure everything is fine." But the humming in Mary's head grew so loud, that it was giving her a headache.

"Yes, that's reassuring. They must be workmen like you said." Sharon moved to the panel of her security system and gave it a little pat. " I'm glad I decided to get this installed a couple years ago."

"After my experience with the movie cast staying at the inn Tom convinced me I should get one, too. Although I haven't yet. I hate feeling as if I need one on our quaint Island, but I guess it would give me peace of mind."

Their friend, Constable Tom Andrews, had been pretty insistent that Mary needed one. Of course, two murders on two separate occasions at the Emerald Inn did make it seem like a wise decision. Just like it was a wise decision to not ignore whoever was at the Vanderhoops.

On the other hand, it wasn't her job to act as some sort of private detective. She would let the police handle this rash of robberies. She was bound and determined to enjoy Christmas. And there was no better place to celebrate than on Martha's Vineyard.

"Okay, I really do need to head home," Mary said as she pulled on her heavy wool coat. Red, for the season. "I'll see you tomorrow for the decorating and lighthouse festivities."

"Sounds good." Sharon tugged on her own full-length parka and gathered up her purse. She armed the security system, and they left the mansion.

"Don't forget to bring me some of that pumpkin bread," Sharon called to Mary as they both headed to their cars. "I'll be your official taste tester."

Mary laughed. "I was planning on it." She waited until Sharon was in her car and the engine was on before she unlocked her own vehicle.

Before she stepped inside her van, though, she felt a nudge to glance again at the Vanderhoop house. Now that it was getting darker, she could see lights shining in several of the windows.

What were the chances that thieves were going to settle into a local's mansion and not even attempt to hide their presence? And the police officer certainly hadn't seemed worried about them being there. She grimaced at herself. Hadn't she just told herself that she was no longer going to be Martha's Vineyard's resident amateur sleuth?

With that she climbed into her driver's seat, started the engine, and cranked up the heat.

Except for the biting chill that blew in from the Atlantic, she loved this time of year.

Despite her peptalk to mind her own business Mary looked one more time at the Vanderhoop house. She absolutely needed to mind her own business. But that still didn't explain the humming of her sixth sense.

"Maybe it's just a hum of holiday cheer," she muttered to herself. She shifted her car into drive and headed back to her inn.

CHAPTER 2

As expected, Starlight pranced at the door as soon as she heard Mary's key in the lock. First, the excited dog greeted Mary with wild swishes of her tail. Then, doing her best Lassie impersonation, she tried to direct Mary to the pantry where her leash waited on a hook.

Mary laughed, following the insistent pup. "All right, all right. I know. I'm a little late."

As if to validate that comment Cindah sauntered out of the kitchen where she had probably been sitting beside her food bowl, staring at the empty dish as if food would magically appear. The cat meowed indignantly and looked thoroughly disgusted. An expression that the fluffy Persian had mastered.

"Let me feed your starving sister," Mary said, as if genuinely negotiating with the German Shepherd, "and then I'll take you on an extra-long walk."

Only five minutes extra, she amended to herself. Now that the sun had gone down the air was getting downright brutal outside.

Mary retrieved a can of tuna from the pantry at the same time she grabbed Starlight's leash. Yes, her pets were spoiled. But she liked spoiling them.

She quickly opened the can and scooped the fish and the juice into Cindah's bowl. The juice was the finicky cat's favorite, so Mary couldn't skimp on that.

The whole time Starlight sat on her haunches, waiting patiently. Mary could swear that the dog understood everything. That was why Mary hadn't mentioned the amount of "extra" time aloud. Starlight would not be impressed with an "extra-long walk", only being an additional five minutes!

Maybe she spent too much time with her pets, Mary pondered with a smile.

Once Cindah was happily lapping at her supper, Mary bundled up, adding a hat and scarf and thick gloves to her festive coat. Then she and Starlight headed out into the cold night air.

As the two of them walked down the quiet street near her inn, Mary focused on the beautiful night. The inky blue sky twinkled with stars, and in the distance, she could hear the crashing of the ocean waves on the shore.

While the houses in West Tisbury were not quite as extravagant as the ones in downtown Edgartown, her neighbors had pulled out all the stops for the season. Wreaths and lights , candles in the windows, and pine boughs decorated each of the large colonials and Cape Cods that lined her street. It was truly a winter wonderland.

Despite the cheerfulness around her, and Starlight's happy sniffing, her mind kept going back to the policeman's warning. A string of robberies. That was pretty unusual for the island.

Mary wondered if she should give Tom a call and ask him about them. Tom was the constable for West Tisbury, but this was a small island, and she was sure he knew about the robberies, even though they weren't happening in his district. At least she didn't think they were happening here in Tisbury. Another reason to call Tom. Just to double check.

Or you could just go home, turn on some Christmas music, and practice making a killer pumpkin bread that would knock the socks off the judges at the baking contest, she told herself. Although killer probably was not the best word choice given her recent track record with murders.

Yes, that was what she should do. Certainly, the police didn't need her help finding the thieves.

Mary ended up making Starlight's walk an extra ten minutes before she headed home and couldn't help but admire her own decorations as they approached the inn. The wreaths and candles in each window looked so lovely—if she did say so herself. She hurried inside and immediately turned on her favorite playlist of Christmas tunes. With Sarah Brightman's voice filling her kitchen, she started to get out her baking supplies and then heard her phone ring.

She had a good idea who was calling even before she answered. Sharon was the only one who regularly used her landline. An old habit left over from calling Aunt Bridget, Mary was sure.

"Hello, did you forget to tell me something about tomorrow?"

Sharon didn't answer her question, instead saying in a tense voice, "I just got a call from my security company. Someone tripped the alarm at the Edgartown house."

"I'll meet you there." Mary hung up and grabbed her coat.

She headed toward the door, only to stop and go back to get Starlight's leash. It might not be a bad idea to show up at Sharon's mansion with a large and intimidating dog at her side. Of course, the way Starlight danced and excitedly wagged her tail at the sight of the leash--twice in one night--she didn't exactly look threatening. But a huge German Shepherd would still probably give a robber some pause, right?

"What do you say, girl? Up for acting as a guard dog?"

Her dog's dark brown eyes shone brightly at the prospect of another adventure. Mary clicked on Starlight's lead , and then headed outside to her van.

When they arrived at Sharon's house, Mary was surprised to see her friend already there, standing outside on the sidewalk. But more shocking was the fact that there was no law enforcement car in sight.

"Did you call the police?" Mary asked as she approached Sharon. It wasn't outside the realm of possibility that her feisty friend had just intended to search the house herself.

So, Mary was relieved when Sharon answered, "The monitoring company for the alarm system placed the call to them. They should be here any minute."

Still, Mary thought, it seemed as if the police should already be there, especially given the fact they knew they were dealing with a string of break-ins in the area.

"Do you think we should go inside?" Sharon asked, pulling her thick coat tighter around herself. Ha! Mary knew Sharon would want to check out the house herself.

"No, I think we should wait. But maybe in one of our cars," she added. The air was even colder now than on her walk.

Before Sharon could agree, Starlight made a low rumble deep in her chest. Mary noticed her dog focused on Sharon's house; her intense stare unwavering.

Mary surveyed the house, trying to see what held Starlight's rapt attention. Then she saw it. Mary was certain that she had seen a shadow pass in front of one of the downstairs windows.

"Did you see that?" Mary asked, her eyes wide.

Sharon frowned. "See what?"

"I swear I just saw somebody moving around in your house."

Sharon peered at the house now, too. After a moment, she said, "I don't see anything. But I'm going to check it out."

Mary immediately grabbed the sleeve of her friend's coat. "No, we shouldn't go in there. What if someone is in there and they're armed? The police will be here soon. We need to wait for them."

Sharon hesitated for a moment, then agreed.

Once again Starlight growled low in her throat, her eyes still locked on the house.

Mary was certain she had seen somebody in there, too, and she couldn't shake the feeling that whoever was in there was watching them back.

Starlight snarled yet again, this one louder and more menacing. But Mary noticed her dog was no longer focused on Sharon's house. She was now staring at the Vanderhoop's house.

Then Mary glimpsed another shadow. But this time, it was outside with them, moving between the two houses. Mary's pulse raced when she realized it was more than just a shadow. It was a dark figure headed toward them! Was this the robber coming to confront them?

The person stepped out into the light of the streetlamps. Mary didn't recognize the man's face, but she did recall the torn jacket. It absolutely was one of the people from earlier.

"Is everything okay, ladies?"

Mary and Sharon exchanged a look before Sharon answered, "We're fine, thank you."

"Just waiting for the police to arrive," Mary added. She got a bad feeling from this guy.

The man nodded, and Mary noticed that he didn't appear overly surprised by the news. In fact, he didn't even ask why they were waiting for the police. Was it because he already knew?

"Have you seen someone prowling around here tonight?" Mary asked, hoping maybe that was why he looked so unfazed by their announcement. Maybe he had seen something. Maybe he'd been outside checking on something suspicious himself. But wouldn't he say that?

He took a step forward. "I haven't seen or heard anything, but I was working in the basement."

"Are you working for the Vanderhoops?"

The man shook his head, then he smiled, although Mary thought the gesture looked a bit stiff as if he was trying to act friendly but couldn't quite pull it off. She also noticed his yellowing teeth and a scar that appeared on his left cheek.

Neither of those things should have mattered. After all, dental care was darned expensive, and a scar didn't exactly label someone as nefarious, but still, his overall look gave her a cold chill--

that had nothing to do with the weather. Starlight seemed to agree, growling again quietly.

"I'm their nephew," he replied. "I thought I would check out the island for the holidays. I've never been here at this time of the year. My aunt and uncle are in Europe for the winter, so they told me to make use of their place."

Again, Mary got the impression that his explanation was flat and as poorly rehearsed as his forced smile. And nephew? He looked rather old, but Mary had no idea how old his aunt and uncle were. Mary had never met the Vanderhoops.

He took another step toward them, and Starlight moved from Mary's side, positioning herself between her owner and the man.

"That's a beautiful dog you have there," the man said, eyeing the shepherd warily. He shoved his hands into the pockets of his worn jacket. The movement made Mary nervous. Did he have a weapon in his pocket?

Starlight began to bare her teeth as she growled quietly. She didn't trust this guy either. And she was an excellent judge of character.

Mary pulled Starlight closer to her, more for the dog's protection than the man's. Something was not right.

To Mary's relief the sound of sirens cut through the freezing night air, and a police car pulled up in front of the mansion. Two officers got out and approached the women. Neither of the men was the one from earlier this evening.

"Are one of you the homeowner?" The bulkier of the two officers asked as they approached.

"I am," Sharon answered. "My house alarm went off earlier, but we think someone is in the house right now."

He nodded. "Okay, we're going to have you wait out here while we take a look around."

Sharon handed him the keys. "I'm not sure if the door is still locked or not."

The officer took them and headed up the porch steps. The second officer suggested that maybe they should wait in their cars, then followed his partner up the stairs.

Mary glanced back to where the man from next-door had been standing. He was gone. She shivered as she stepped closer to Sharon.

"I wonder why he left?" Mary said, kept her voice hushed in case he still was lurking about. She gestured for them to go sit in her van. She had to admit waiting in her vehicle did seem safer. And warmer.

"Because he didn't want to talk to the police would be my guess," Sharon said flatly. "I don't believe for a minute the Vanderhoops would let that guy stay in their place—nephew or not."

As soon as they were settled in the van. Mary turned up the heat, not speaking for a moment until the rush of hot air thawed her frozen skin a little.

"Do you think we should mention him to these officers?" Mary asked.

"Definitely. He did come out from between our houses. He could have been trying to get in my back door."

"Or he could have already been inside--and left through your back door."

"Well, Starlight didn't like him, that's for sure," Sharon reached to where the Shepherd sat in between the two women and scratched her neck. Starlight barely acknowledged the affectionate touch, still on alert.

Mary was glad she had followed her gut and brought Starlight with her tonight. Even though the "nephew" hadn't done anything threatening she wasn't sure he wouldn't have, and she felt certain that the large Shepherd had been the main factor in him keeping his distance.

"Do you have any way of contacting the Vanderhoops?" Mary asked.

Sharon shook her head. "I haven't spoken to them in years. Even when Edwin and I lived in this house, we never mingled with them. I always got the feeling they considered themselves better than us."

Mary blinked in shock. "Wasn't Edwin from one of the oldest families in the Vineyard?"

"The second oldest." Sharon tilted her head with a pointed smile at the Vanderhoop mansion. "And I'll let you guess who the oldest family is."

"Ahh," Mary said knowingly.

"Which is exactly why I don't buy for a second that the guy over there is a part of their family."

Mary didn't buy it either.

Both women jumped as there was a sharp rap on the passenger side window. Starlight barked, adding to the tense moment.

But it was just the officers.

After taking a moment to gather herself, Sharon opened the window.

"Sorry," the larger officer said. "We're done with our walk through. We didn't find anyone in the house or see anything unusual."

That had been quick. Had they really searched the whole house?

If Sharon wondered the same thing, she didn't say anything, instead asking, "So, what could have set off the alarm, then?"

"It happens sometimes," the larger officer said seemingly unconcerned. "Or maybe you did it yourself by accident? Or maybe it was an animal?" He leveled a look at Starlight.

Sharon shook her head. "I wasn't even here, and I don't have any pets."

"Yes, this is my dog," Mary said. "And we only got here after the alarm went off."

The officer shrugged. "The place looks fine. No signs of anyone messing with the locks or windows."

Mary frowned at the men. Their lack of concern seemed odd, especially after the other officer had bothered to come door-to-door to warn the homeowners about burglaries.

"Everything looks perfectly safe," the shorter officer said, clearly confused by both women's lack of relief.

"But the other officer told us there have been several break ins in this area," Sharon posited.

The larger officer glanced at his partner. "Other officer?"

"Yes, an officer came to my door earlier tonight and told us the police department was making homeowners aware that there had been some robberies in this area recently."

The officers exchanged another look.

"Ma'am, there have been a couple robberies, but the police have not gone door-to-door to share that information."

It was Mary and Sharon's turn to glance at each other.

"Can you describe the man from earlier?"

Both Mary and Sharon told them everything they could recall. The officers still looked baffled.

"I think you should really talk to the man staying in that house," Sharon added, pointing out the window to the correct house.

"Why is that?" This time, the shorter officer spoke before the taller one, although Mary didn't get the sense that he believed their story either.

"I know the Vanderhoops, and I find it very hard to believe this person is the relative he claims to be," Sharon retorted, holding back frustration.

"And why is that?" the shorter one asked. Apparently, that was why the taller one did most of the talking. This officer seemed to have a limited repertoire of questions.

"The Vanderhoops are very old money. This guy does not give off an old money vibe," Sharon said.

The officers didn't look impressed with that explanation, but the larger one nodded. "All right, we'll go talk to him."

"Thank you," Sharon said, although she didn't manage to sound any more sincere than the officer had.

The two men headed over to the neighboring house. Both Mary and Sharon watched to see if the guy even answered the door when the policemen knocked. To her surprise, the man did--and he invited them inside.

But almost as quickly as they had searched Sharon's house, the officers were back.

"He's a nephew of the Vanderhoops. And he has the keys to the place," the large officer said as if having a set of keys was airtight proof that the man belonged there.

Sharon gave the men a dubious look.

"Listen," the large officer said, clearly growing frustrated with the two women. "He even says he can show us emails with his uncle to prove he arranged to be here this week. He's just here with his kids to enjoy the Island's Christmas festivities."

Mary frowned. So, having kids proved he wasn't a shady character? But she didn't ask that. Instead she questioned, "But what about the person impersonating a police officer. Isn't that worrisome?"

"I admit, it's strange, but ultimately, it doesn't seem terribly threatening," the larger officer said. "I mean, it sounds like he was actually just telling you to be careful and keep your house locked up."

Sharon made an irritated noise but said nothing more. Neither did Mary. She got the distinct feeling that both officers thought she and Sharon were just kooky and nosy women, probably scared of their own shadows.

"All I can tell you, ladies, is that the house is clear and everything looks perfectly safe. But if you have any other problems give us a call back." With that, both officers nodded a goodbye and headed back to their vehicle.

"Fat chance--I'd rather call the Ghostbusters before I called them again," Sharon muttered as she watched them leave.

They both remained silent for a moment, neither of them quite processing what had just happened.

"If that wasn't an Edgartown officer earlier, then who was he?" Sharon finally verbalized out loud what they were both thinking. "And why would he tell us about a string of robberies?"

Mary shook her head. "That's a great question."

CHAPTER 3

"Will you come inside with me?" Sharon asked after a moment. "I want to look around myself. Those two Barney Fifes wouldn't have any idea if anything was missing. Plus, I want to double check the alarm and reset it."

"Absolutely." Mary reached for Starlight's leash. Her guard dog was definitely going with them, too. She didn't have any more faith in the police officers than Sharon did. Someone could still be hiding in there.

As soon as they stepped inside the mansion, Mary absolutely knew someone had tried to break into the house tonight. She could feel it, although she also got the sense that they hadn't been here long enough to steal anything.

But someone had been in here, for sure. Both she and Starlight had seen that shadow in the front window.

Mary wasn't sure if she should tell Sharon about her feelings, however. Her friend was already stressed out about preparing for the tour--not to mention dealing with all the emotions that seeing the house decorated again for the holidays would stir up in her. Did she really need to worry about an intruder on top of all that? Especially when whoever tried to break in tonight now knew she had an alarm system. It seemed highly unlikely that they would try again.

"I don't see anything missing or out of place," Sharon said as they walked through the house.

"Well, that's a relief," Mary said. She knew a burglar could clean up in this house. There had to be hundreds of thousands of dollars' worth of antiques, art and sterling silver in this home.

They headed back to the front foyer, and Sharon checked the alarm. "Everything looks fine with this, too."

Mary had no doubt. The alarm was exactly what had stopped the potential burglar.

"I guess I can just re-arm it, and we can head out."

Mary nodded, making the decision to keep her intuition to herself. Her intuition, gut, feeling, psychic ability, or whatever she chose to call it in the moment, told her that no one would be back tonight. Hopefully, they wouldn't be back at all.

As Sharon started to punch in the code, Mary noticed that Starlight was no longer with them. Where was she? Her dog was usually her shadow, especially in an unfamiliar place.

"Wait a minute!" Mary tapped Sharon on her shoulder. "We seem to have lost Starlight."

Sharon looked compassionately toward Mary, knowing this was unusual behavior for the dog, too.

Mary checked in the living room and dining room. She finally located Starlight sitting directly in front of the back door, staring at it.

"What is that silly dog doing?" Sharon asked with a slight chuckle.

Before she even thought better of it, Mary replied, "This is the door the intruder left through."

Well, so much for keeping Sharon in the dark.

"What? Are you sure?"

"Yes," Mary nodded, noting that her friend didn't even question how Mary knew that information, just whether she was certain. Sharon had more confidence in Mary's abilities than she did herself.

"I could actually feel that someone had definitely been in here tonight, but I didn't want to worry you," Mary admitted, feeling guilty now for keeping the information to herself.

Sharon waved Mary's regretful tone away. "I appreciate that, but we need to call the police again. The situation is serious. Someone did break in. And it had to be that guy next door. I mean why else was he behind the house?"

Mary went to the door and unlocked it. She studied the lock mechanism but couldn't see any marks that looked like it had been tampered with.

She sighed. "I don't see anything unusual with the lock. And obviously those two officers didn't see anything either. They're not going to believe us without any physical signs of a break-in. It's not like they are going to just accept that I can sense someone broke in."

If the officers thought she was a kook already, telling them that she just knew about the attempted break-in would probably make them more focused on getting her committed than actually searching for the burglar.

Sharon agreed but looked defeated. "Yeah, I suspect you're right."

Mary closed and locked the door. "If it's any consolation, I'm not getting the feeling that the robbers will be back." She didn't add, "tonight."

Sharon sighed. "Well, that's something at least." She walked to the kitchen island to where Mary had left her half full martini from before. Sharon picked up the glass and swigged it down in one swallow.

"I don't suppose you got any impression of who actually tried to rob me?" Sharon asked. "Not that I need your psychic abilities to have my own suspicions."

"No, I can't see anything about that, but I also have my suspicions, and they're the same as yours." Mary glanced at the kitchen window in the direction of the Vanderhoop house.

Sharon followed her gaze.

"But unfortunately the police believe him. And they don't believe us."

Sharon twirled her empty martini glass stem several times with her fingertips. "Well, I am definitely going to keep an eye on that guy."

Mary looked at Sharon with a reassuring smile "And I'm going to be calling Tom tomorrow." This might not be Tom's district, but Mary suspected that the Edgartown police would be more willing to listen to Constable Andrews than they would be to her.

The next morning, Mary made a call to Tom.

"Mary," he greeted her, clearly happy to hear from her, but not surprised. She hoped that was because he considered them friends, and not because he had just come to expect her to be having some sort of legal issue.

"How are you?" he asked with a bit of concern.

"I'm doing well. Well, mostly well. I'm actually calling to see if you've heard any buzz about robberies in Edgartown."

"I did have a beer with the sheriff over there a couple nights ago. He did mention that crime in their area was up a bit, but he didn't go into any specifics. Why do you ask?"

"I'm not sure if you knew that Sharon owns a house over on North Water Street."

Tom let out a soft whistle. "No, I didn't. I had no idea that I had been hobnobbing with a member of the Martha's Vineyard elite."

Mary laughed. "Don't let her hear you calling her that. She's not a big fan of Edgartown's elite. She actually inherited the house from her husband." Mary didn't bother to clarify which husband. "Anyway, we believe that someone tried to break into the house last night. We called the police, but they couldn't find any signs of an attempt to break in."

"But you know someone tried?" Tom phrased his response in the form of a question, but Mary knew it wasn't really a question. Just like

Sharon, Constable Tom Andrews didn't seem to have any doubts about Mary's psychic abilities.

"Yes," she said, without hesitation.

"Do you know who it was?"

"I'm not sure, but I have a strong suspicion."

Tom was quiet for a moment. "Suspicion? Or are you certain?"

"I'm not sure," she said honestly. "But there is someone staying at the house next to Sharon's. This guy says he's a relative of the people who own the house. But something about his story doesn't feel right to me."

Tom was silent again for a moment. "Okay, I'll give Sheriff Wilks a call. Try to feel him out a little bit about the criminal activity in that area, and I'll see if I can get him to personally check on the guy staying next door."

"Also, we had someone stop by Sharon's mansion claiming to be a cop. He warned us about several home burglaries in the area. But when we told the officers about it last night, they said that none of their officers had been going door-to-door."

"Okay, that's very weird. I'll definitely ask Wilks about that, too."

"Thank you, Tom. Will you be at the Edgartown Harbor Lighthouse lighting tomorrow night?"

"Now, I think missing that is actually against the law."

Mary laughed. "Then I hope I'll see you there."

"I look forward to it."

**

The Peabody Mansion was bustling when Mary arrived at noon. There were so many crew members scurrying around with arms full of decorations, Mary had a hard time locating Sharon.

In fact, she didn't see her, but rather heard her.

"No, no, no. That garland goes on the staircase!" It seemed to Mary that her friend's cry carried an uncharacteristic frustration which made her usually husky voice sound like a shriek.

Mary followed the sound of Sharon's harried shout to the grand staircase, where she found her friend surrounded by a sea of fresh evergreen garlands and wreaths and a group of very stressed-looking decorators.

Sharon held a martini glass in one hand while waving wildly with the other. Mary knew things were not going well if her friend already had a cocktail by noon.

"It can't just be thrown up there. The swags must be even, and the wreaths centered."

"Hey," Mary called carefully, not wanting to agitate her friend even more. "What's going on?"

Sharon spotted Mary, and a look of relief washed over her face. She stepped over the garlands and grabbed Mary's arm, tugging her into the relative privacy of the dining room.

"Mary." She sighed, its resonance tinged with panic. "These people don't seem to have a clue what they're doing. Everything has been a disaster."

Mary glanced around the dining room, which appeared to already be completed. The room's fireplace was fully adorned, its mantlepiece draped with lush garlands of fresh evergreens and embellished with glistening beads and ribbons. Tall, white tapered candles in antique silver candlesticks were lit and cast the room in a warm, inviting glow.

The dining room table was a masterpiece in and of itself, dressed in a crisp, white damask tablecloth intricately embroidered with golden threads. Fine china dishes with patterns of holly and ivy were arranged as place settings alongside sparkling crystal stemware and polished silver cutlery.

The centerpiece was an enormous, yet exquisite, arrangement of deep, red roses, white hydrangeas, and sprigs of evergreen and holly. And in the corner of the dining room, near the fireplace sat an elegantly decorated eight-foot tree, glittering with gold and silver ornaments, delicate blown glass balls, and twinkling white lights. Strands of tinsel had been meticulously draped over the boughs, reminding Mary of Christmases long ago.

"Sharon, this room couldn't be any more perfect. I think the decorators are doing a fabulous job."

Sharon took a deep breath and surveyed the room. After a moment, some of her agitation faded.

"This does look beautiful," she conceded. "Am I getting too worked up?"

Mary smiled sympathetically at her friend. "Well, you know how you always tell me you have no idea how I deal with all of the Bridezillas when I'm catering?"

Sharon winced. "Oh my God, am I being a Tourzilla?"

Mary chuckled. "I think you just want everything to be perfect. But don't worry, everything looks amazing."

Sharon smiled gratefully. She scanned the room again. "It does. I guess I'm just getting into my own head too much." She sipped her martini and pulled in a calming breath.

Mary squeezed her friend's arm reassuringly. "It's totally understandable. This is a lot for you. But we will get everything done, and it will be stunning."

"Thank you, Mary. I don't know what I would do without you."

"That's what friends are for. Now, put me to work."

Sharon smiled, then gestured toward the front living room. "I'll have you oversee the main Christmas tree. I don't think I can control my OCD enough to work on that one."

Mary laughed. "Knowing your weaknesses is half the battle. Don't worry, I'm on it."

Almost three hours later, Mary and her two other helpers, Carla and Lillian, stood back to admire their handiwork. The two women looked as tired and as proud as Mary felt. They had created a masterpiece if Mary did say so herself.

"I don't think we could get one more ornament onto that tree," Carla noted, shaking her head at the grandeur of the house's focal point.

Every inch of the enormous tree was adorned with an assortment of exquisite ornaments. Sparkling crystal baubles, hand-blown glass figures, and delicate porcelain balls hung from every branch and reflected the glow of hundreds of sparkling lights. It really was spectacular!

"I have to admit, it was nerve-wracking to be handling all of those old and fragile ornaments," Lilian said, wiping her sweaty brow like a surgeon who'd just done a particularly complicated surgery. "I bet some of those ornaments are older than my grandparents."

"Older than my grandparents," Sharon said from behind them as she entered the room. She stopped, taking in their painstaking work. "This is fantastic. Just beautiful."

Mary could've sworn she saw the glistening of tears in her friend's eyes as she admired the gorgeous tree. But if her eyes had grown dewy, Sharon quickly hid them behind a wide smile.

"It's just how I imagined it. Now, I'm sure you are all starving. I ordered food for everyone. It's only pizza and wings, but there's plenty for everyone. It's all set up in the kitchen."

Mary smiled at her friend, glad to see that even though this whole event was emotionally taxing, Sharon seemed to be enjoying it a bit more.

Carla and Lillian didn't need any more of an invitation than that as they happily left the room in search of the food.

Mary moved to stand beside her friend. They both continued to admire the tree.

"Edwin would be so delighted by all of this," Sharon said softly.

Mary slipped an arm around the older woman, giving her a comforting squeeze. Neither of them said anything for a moment, they just basked in the beauty of the Christmas tree and all the spectacular decorations.

Sharon sniffed and then straightened. "We better get in the kitchen and get something to eat. This is a hungry crowd. I don't think the pizza will last long."

Mary followed Sharon toward the scent of pepperoni pizza and buffalo sauce. She had wanted to say more to her, to comfort her, because she knew how bittersweet all of this was for her friend. But when she heard Sharon enter the kitchen, and cheerfully and sincerely thank all of her decorating crew---who all applauded Sharon back—Mary knew that this was exactly what her friend needed. It was better to create this new memory than to get caught up in memories of the past.

Mary watched the joyful gathering in front of her. The crew munched on their food and chattered excitedly about their hard work. This was what the holidays were all about. Enjoying the company of others—whether it was family, friends, or a group of relative strangers who had just survived decorating boot camp.

Suddenly a movement out of the corner of her eye pulled her attention away from the feasting crew. Outside the window, she saw the man from next door. He was looking at Sharon's house, and his expression was less than joyous. He caught Mary's gaze and stared back at her with cold, dark eyes.

CHAPTER 4

Once the impromptu pizza party was finished and all the workers had been paid and sent on their merry way, Mary and Sharon collapsed onto the settee in the sitting room.

"Even with all the help, this has been exhausting," Sharon groaned.

"It really was exhausting," Mary agreed. "But the hard work was worth it. You are going to have the most stunning house on the tour."

Sharon looked around and nodded approvingly. "I think you're right. Let the Gossip Gang try to find a flaw in this place."

They were both silent for a moment, then Sharon said, "I asked two of the crewmen who were here today to come back and stay in the house for the next few nights. I've been friends with their mother for years, and I trust them. I just don't think that I should leave the house empty after what happened yesterday."

Mary sat up, feeling a wave of relief. "I think that's a great idea. And I did get in touch with Tom this morning. He said he was going to contact Edgartown's sheriff, just to see what's been going on around here."

"Oh, that's good. I'm sure Tom will have more success getting to the bottom of things than we would."

Mary put her hand on Sharon's shoulder, again debating how much she should say to her friend. She wasn't sure if she should mention that she'd seen the neighbor watching her house today. That weird neighbor was really the last thing Sharon needed to think about right now, that was for sure.

But Sharon beat her to the punch. "All day, I kept catching glimpses of that guy next-door, staring over here. I don't care what those officers thought about him last night, that guy is a shady character."

"Yeah, I saw him, too. When everybody was in the kitchen eating."

Sharon shook her head. "I hope Tom can find out something. Or at least get the sheriff to investigate a little more."

Mary agreed. She genuinely did not want to play Nancy Drew, but her curiosity was getting the better of her. Who was that guy? And what was he up to?

Mary and Sharon relaxed for a little while longer but soon decided they better head over to the Edgartown Harbor Lighthouse. Even though they were tired, they didn't want to miss the event.

When they arrived there were already crowds of people gathering, locals and tourists alike. The excited sounds of children and the laughter of adults echoed over the sound of the waves in the harbor.

Mary and Sharon walked up the pathway leading to the lighthouse. Lanterns lined either side of the winding trail, casting warm and flickering shadows on the ground. Ahead of them, they could hear the sound of a live band on the stage erected just for the event. Upbeat Christmas music made the air feel alive.

Mary loved the energy all around them. It drove away the negative feeling that lingered from that strange man in the Vanderhoop's house. Soon, she wasn't thinking about the creep at all. She found herself humming along with the song the band was playing, Here Comes Santa Claus.

A group of small children bundled up in snowsuits danced to the tune, giddy over the impending visit from the jolly man in red. The kids themselves looked like elves with their winter hats and rosy cheeks.

Both Mary and Sharon grinned at their antics. Mary could vividly remember that feeling of glorious anticipation. It was magic!

"Do you want a cup of hot chocolate?" Mary asked, spotting the vendor.

"I suppose we should keep this event wholesome," Sharon said with a disappointed sigh.

Mary shook her head indulgently at her friend. "Maybe they have chocolate martinis."

"I wish," Sharon grinned, her longing obvious.

"You go ahead and save us a spot, and I'll get the hot chocolate."

"Ok." Sharon had already scoped out a spot with the best view.

Mary jumped on the end of the long line, everyone eager for warm drinks and decorated sugar cookies. As she waited, she found herself enjoying the people-watching. Many parents looked more than a little exhausted from dealing with kids who were hopped up on Christmas excitement. Older couples who had expressions that said they were glad to be past the age of having to rein in the wild children. Even teenagers, trying to play cool seemed to be caught up in the Christmas cheer, too. Mary loved everything about this. Of course, she could people-watch all day--that was just part of her curious nature.

The young couple ahead of her in line caught her attention. Maybe in her mid-twenties the woman pressed against her boyfriend or husband, clearly trying to keep warm. They smiled fondly at each other and sneaked a quick kiss.

Mary smiled. To be young and in love. As she continued to watch them, she saw someone in a bulky dark coat, with a hood pulled up to shield from the cold, accidentally bump into them.

"Hey!" the young man called out, looping an arm protectively around his date.

Mary heard the person give a mumbling apology as they hurried past, their gait uneven. Maybe one of the other vendors was offering something stronger than hot chocolate and mulled cider. The person--she got the impression he was male even though she couldn't see his face-- seemed to be a little tipsy.

"Well, if it isn't my favorite innkeeper and caterer."

Mary turned from watching the hooded figure amble away to see Nathan Stewart standing beside her. Was it possible that this man could look even more handsome than usual in his dark blue peacoat and knit cap?

Yes, yes, it was.

He sported a beard, which was new from the last time she saw him. His facial hair made him look even more ruggedly attractive. Although she doubted that was why he had grown it. The new addition was probably more of a defense against the cold weather than a fashion statement. But it did look good.

"Hi Nathan," she responded, hoping she hadn't been openly admiring him for too long. "Merry Christmas!"

If she had been ogling him a tad too long, he didn't show that he noticed. "Merry Christmas to you! I like your red coat. Perfect for the season."

She started to thank him when he added "Red is your color. It looks beautiful with your hair."

As far as compliments went it wasn't the most extravagant one, she had ever received, but that didn't matter. Her cheeks still warmed at the flattery.

"Thank you," she managed to say, without sounding too flustered. Or at least she hoped she hadn't. "I like the beard. Very New England chic."

"Part of my winter wardrobe," he laughed as he rubbed his fingers over the coarse hair and confirmed her suspicions.

Mary looked away from him to realize that she was the next one to put in an order. "Can I get you hot chocolate?"

"How about I get you hot chocolate?"

She smiled. "That's nice of you, but I'm also getting Sharon one."

"Perfect," he said with an easy smile. "I was planning on getting her one, too. So, this works out great."

Mary suspected if some other guy had said this to her she would find it a bit contrived, and maybe even a little too smooth. But Nathan always came across as absolutely sincere. That was one of the things she liked best about him. He was a genuinely nice person. Of course, it didn't hurt that he was ridiculously handsome, too.

He ordered three hot chocolates and three snickerdoodles. She smiled slightly because she had always preferred snickerdoodles to sugar cookies.

The young woman hustling around the vending booth quickly gathered up their order and Nathan paid. Mary took one of the cocoas and the cookies, while Nathan grabbed the other two drinks.

"Thank you," Mary said.

"Happy to do it. It's my way of sort of inviting myself to join you and Sharon."

"Well, you didn't need to bribe us. We're happy to have you join us," Mary replied with a flutter in her chest. Nathan's company was more than enough treat.

Wow, the lovebirds from earlier must be getting to her.

As they picked their way through the crowd searching for Sharon, Mary thought of something. "I just realized I don't actually know anything about your family. Are you planning to spend the holidays with them?"

Nathan shook his head. "It's just me, my mom, and my sister. My sister lives in Maryland with her family, and my mother is going down there to spend the holiday with them. I was invited, but I hate to miss Christmas on the Island. Plus, the week between Christmas and New Year's is a surprisingly busy time for me."

"I'm sure a lot of cheese is eaten in that particular week." Mary's smile faded to a pensive glance. "Still, it must be kind of lonely to be away from family."

"It's not bad. I have lots of friends and all the events happening on the Island make it pretty Christmasy. What about you? Do you have family coming in?" Nathan turned to look at Mary with a warm smile.

"My dad will be here in a few days. He's actually the only family I have. Although I do consider Sharon to be my family as well."

"That'll be nice."

Mary considered inviting him to her Christmas dinner, but she wasn't sure if that would seem too forward.

Then the hooded figure from earlier caught her attention. The figure stood at the edge of the gathered crowd and seemed to be watching everyone. Assessing them. Suddenly, the person didn't seem tipsy at all. He was too focused for that.

Mary still couldn't make out any features, and from their slight build she couldn't even tell for sure if they were male or female. And just like that the faint humming in her head was back.

Mary fought back the urge to groan. Couldn't she just have one night off from her abilities?

Nathan must have noticed her pained look because he asked, "Mary, are you okay?"

She managed a reassuring smile.

"But do you happen to recognize that person?" Mary pointed to the hooded figure as subtly as she could.

Nathan peered in the direction she indicated, then his brow furrowed.

"No, I don't think so. But they look a little sketchy."

Mary nodded. "Yeah, I saw them earlier when I was waiting in line. They bumped into the couple in front of me and my first thought was that something was off with them."

They both watched as the figure moved into the crowd, occasionally stumbling into attendees as Mary had just described.

"Maybe they just did a little too much partying before they came here!" Nathan offered as he strained a little to track the figure.

"Yeah, I'm sure that's probably what it is." But she wasn't sure.

"Oh, I see Sharon!" Nathan reached for Mary's arm, and she was relieved by the distraction.

They headed in the older woman's direction.

Not-so-subtly widening her eyes with excitement, Sharon grinned when she saw who was walking with Mary.

"Oh, I see you were picking up men while in line. I was wondering what was taking so long."

Nathan laughed and held out a hot chocolate to his less-than-tactful friend. "I think technically, I picked her up."

Sharon looked even more intrigued. "Even better."

"This is a great location," Mary added, trying to change the subject.

Sharon took the bait, although her smirk said that she knew what Mary was trying to do.

"Years of experience. You want to be far enough back so you can see the whole lighthouse light up. But not so far back that you don't get the full experience of how impressive it is and can't see the guest speaker." Sharon explained.

Nathan was impressed. "You've definitely put some thought into this."

Sharon nodded proudly. "Yes, I have!"

Mary was listening, but her gaze scanned the crowd, trying to spot that figure again. Even as she told herself to let it go. She was here to enjoy herself. Period.

"I found you," a gravelly voice erupted from beside her.

Mary turned to see Tom. Tonight, the constable wore a long wool coat with a red scarf and a tweed flat cap. His whole outfit looked very festive, but still a bit wrinkled and a little shabby. Mary had come to think of this as his signature style.

Mary hugged the older man who smelled like strong coffee and peppermint. It was nice, actually. "I'm glad you found us."

Tom moved to give Sharon a hug as well and then he shook Nathan's hand.

"I wasn't going to miss the chance to hang out with my favorite psychic friend," Tom pronounced with a wink.

Mary closed her eyes briefly and fought the urge to groan. Had he really just said that? Tom was usually a little more subtle than that. Had he been hanging around Sharon too long?

Mary didn't even risk a look at Nathan. If he had been even remotely interested in her Mary was sure he wasn't now. Nathan didn't seem like the type to put much stock in psychic abilities.

Fortunately, Mary was saved having to respond by the crackling of a microphone over the loudspeaker.

A booming voice filled the night air, and the crowd's chatter quieted down. The voice belonged to the Edgartown Mayor who, along with several others, was standing on a makeshift stage at the base of the lighthouse. Mary assumed these other people were also town officials.

"Good evening, everyone. Welcome to the annual lighting of the Edgartown Harbor Lighthouse. We're so glad to see such a large turnout tonight."

The crowd cheered, and some of the agitations that had tightened Mary's chest at Tom's comment was replaced by the excited energy stirring around her. Plus, Nathan hadn't hightailed it out of there at the unexpected reveal of Mary's abilities.

He still stood right next to her, so close she could occasionally feel the brush of his arm against hers. All his attention seemed focused on the ceremony. He had a happy smile on his face. Maybe he hadn't even heard Tom's comment. The band and the crowd were loud, so probably he hadn't. She could hope anyway.

"As you all know," the Mayor continued, "this is a beloved tradition here on the Island, and we're thrilled to have so many locals and visitors with us tonight. And we're equally thrilled to have a very special guest to help us with the lighting as well. I'm pleaded to introduce the author of the bestselling novel,

The Lightkeeper's Daughter, the Vineyard's very own Ms. Georgia Williams."

Mary knew that the successful author called Martha's Vineyard her home, but Mary had never seen her. Ms. Williams was known to be a bit of a recluse. But Mary had read several of her books and had enjoyed them all.

Georgia Williams was a petite, older woman with wild and frizzy gray hair and reading glasses that kept slipping down her nose. She looked more as if she should have been have teaching spellcasting at Hogwarts than the guest speaker at a Christmas lighting ceremony.

But her brief speech was excellent, talking about her love of the Island and sharing a few of her best holiday memories. It was clear listening to her that she was a natural-born storyteller. And by the time she finished, Mary's worries about Nathan thinking that she was a crazy eccentric, and even the strange feelings about the stumbling hooded person, were gone, replaced by the good feelings of Ms. Williams' great holiday stories.

The mayor returned to the podium to start the buildup of the excitement which always happened counting down to the illumination of the lights.

When the lighthouse ultimately glowed to life in a dazzling arrray of twinkling lights that illuminated the white cylindrical building and sparkled off the waves of the harbor, the crowd cheered. And Mary no longer thought about anything other than drinking her cocoa and singing along with the band who had started their Christmas songs.

Unfortunately, the Christmas bliss of the moment didn't last when Tom tugged at Mary's sleeve and nodded toward a quieter place away from the crowd.

"Let's talk. I got some information from Sheriff Wilks."

Although Mary wasn't quite ready to give up her holiday euphoria, she nodded, then turned apologetically to Nathan. "I'm sorry, I have to speak with Constable Andrews for a moment. I'm glad we ran into each other. Thank you for the cocoa and snickerdoodle." She waved the plastic-wrapped cookie that she hadn't even eaten yet.

"My pleasure," he smiled, then his expression grew more serious.

'Uh-oh, here comes the question about the psychic comment. Thanks, Tom' Mary thought, still confused why he would say such a thing.

"I don't suppose you're planning to attend the Christmas parade tomorrow?"

Mary didn't respond for a moment, so sure the woo-woo question was coming that she couldn't quite shift gears.

But finally her brain kicked in. "Oh, yes. Yes, I'm going."

"Great, maybe we can catch up there."

It wasn't exactly an official invitation, but Mary would take it. "Definitely!"

"I'll be there, too. I'll look for you."

Mary grinned. "Great."

But then, to her further surprise, he hugged her.

"Good luck with your talk with the Constable. I hope you can help him with your abilities."

Mary wanted to groan. He had heard after all.

Before she could respond, he had moved to say goodbye to the others.

"Let's go get a cup of coffee, and I'll fill you in on my chat with Wilks," Tom said to both Mary and Sharon.

Mary linked her arm through her friend's. Hmm, this sounded like it was going to be interesting.

CHAPTER 5

"The inn looks beautiful," Tom said as he got out of his beat-up old sedan. Tom's car was a bit like the man himself. Maybe a little worse for wear, but still solid and reliable.

They had decided it would probably be better to just head back to Mary's Inn and have coffee there. All the restaurants in Edgartown were probably going to have lines of people waiting to get a seat. All the lighting attendees were very likely thinking the same thing. Food and drinks and getting warm.

"Thank you, Tom" Mary paused to admire the outside decor. "I decided to get everything done early so I could actually enjoy it. That's exactly why I also didn't take any catering jobs for all of December. I just wanted to have a relaxed holiday season."

"And leave it to me to mess all that up for you," Sharon interjected, joining them to head up the walkway.

Mary looked quizzically at her friend. "How did you mess that up for me?"

"Putting you to work at the mansion. Getting you involved in some shady business going on in town." Sharon shot a look toward Tom. "At least, I'm going to assume there's some shady business going on since you want to chat with us."

Mary unlocked her front door, and they all stepped into the thankfully warm foyer. Starlight greeted the group with her happy dance. And they, in turn, greeted her.

Mary made a face at Sharon as she took their coats. "You know I'm more than happy to help you with the mansion. And you didn't get me involved in any shady business." Whatever was going on in Edgartown had found them. "But let me get some coffee started before we get to that."

Mary hung up their coats on the coat tree by the door, then headed toward the kitchen.

"Sorry girl, I think tonight is just an 'explore the backyard' night," Mary told her eager pup as she headed to the back door. If Starlight was disappointed by the lack of walk this evening, she didn't show it and readily went outside to happily sniff and do her usual perimeter check of the yard. Starlight was ever hopeful that there would be a squirrel that needed to be chased away.

Tom took a seat at the kitchen table while Mary got the coffee pot going. Sharon, of course, headed straight to the pantry where Mary kept the makings for her friend's martinis.

Shortly, Sharon returned with her beloved martini, settled herself at the table, and took a sip of the Grey Goose and olives, she sighed with pleasure. "Now that warms the insides."

Tom smiled wryly. "I'm sure it does."

Sharon grinned unapologetically. "Okay, so give us the skinny. What did you find out from Sheriff Wilks?"

Mary glanced at them but continued to slice the loaf of pumpkin bread that she had made this morning. Yes, she wanted to know what Tom found out, but she might as well take advantage of taste testers while she had them here.

"He said that there have been a couple home robberies in Edgartown over the past week. The thieves seem to be targeting houses they know will be empty in the winter. But that isn't what the crime spree is."

Mary stopped slicing the bread to turn towards the Constable. "There's another crime spree?"

"Yes, apparently Edgartown has a sudden abundance of pickpockets."

Sharon set down her martini glass. "Pickpockets? Is that still a thing?"

Tom accepted the steaming mug of coffee that Mary held out to him. With his other hand he gave her a thumbs up thanks. "Apparently, it is."

Mary joined them at the table, setting the plate of pumpkin bread in the center. Sharon immediately reached for a slice.

"I guess with all the gatherings for the holidays, it would be actually easy pickings," Sharon said dryly. She took a bite of the pumpkin bread and moaned in bliss. "Oh, this is going to win the baking contest, hands-down."

"Do you think so? I wasn't sure if pumpkin was too much of a Thanksgiving flavor."

With a look of pure nirvana, Sharon reassured her friend. "No, this is so good, no one will even think about it."

Mary took a piece and tasted it. It was, in fact, delicious, but she thought she could do better. The ratio of cinnamon to cloves wasn't quite right. And this bread needed to be perfect. One of her rival caterers, Angela Jordan, who owned Divine Dishes, had won the last two years in a row. Mary hoped this was her year.

Of course, that really wasn't the main concern right now.

"Did Sheriff Wilks have any thoughts on who the police imposter might've been?" Mary asked.

Tom finished taking a sip of his coffee, then shook his head. "No, he's not sure. Our best guess is that it was the guy who has been doing the home break-ins. He was probably seeing if you would be there over the holidays."

"He did ask if I was staying there" Sharon noted, swirling her martini thoughtfully. Then she looked at Mary. "And I did say I wasn't staying there nights. And then the alarm goes off that very night. Not long after we left."

"But you also told him you have a security system, so he knew you did."

"That's true, so it doesn't seem likely he would try to break in. So, who did try to?" Sharon tapped the side of her glass.

"I read the report you gave the officers that night," Tom said. "But tell me about him again."

"He was young--maybe early twenties. And very thin. Lanky," Sharon recalled.

Mary considered that. The strange person at the lighting had the same build.

"Really, he looked almost too young to be an officer," Sharon continued, "although I didn't think about that at the time."

Mary's brain began to hum.

"I think you really need to look into the man who is staying at the Vanderhoops!" Mary suddenly stated with authority.

Tom studied her. "You mentioned that, and I did talk to Sheriff Wilks about him. He said he went there himself earlier today, and the man had the house keys and even had texts on his phone about making arrangements to be there. Wilks said they were from Arthur Vanderhoop."

Mary frowned. "Arthur?"

She got up to let Starlight back inside. After sniffing all of Mary's guests again, Starlight settled on her dog bed next to the table.

"Arthur and Clara Vanderhoop. They own the house," Sharon clarified.

"Are they old enough to have a nephew the age of that guy?" Mary asked, taking a seat again.

Sharon shrugged, then nodded. "I would say so. Arthur and Clara must be in their mid-seventies by now. Although, I've never met any of their siblings, so I can't say for sure."

Mary leaned back in her chair, pondering that. "Well, texts can certainly be faked. And there are ways to get the house keys."

"I agree," Tom said, "but Sheriff Wilks seems to believe the man."

Mary wondered if Sheriff Wilks met the same person she had met. Everything about that man had screamed shifty. Yet everyone seemed to believe him.

"Well, I guess it's just as well I asked Doug and Kevin Sullivan to stay at the Peabody Mansion. I think I'll tell them to keep an eye on the Vanderhoop house while they're there, too," Sharon decided.

Tom made a slight noise that sounded like a snort that he knew he should try to suppress.

"What?" Sharon asked, narrowing her eyes to look at him.

"Doug and Kevin are great guys, but Sherlock Holmes and Watson they are not."

Mary did a better job of suppressing her own chuckle. It was true, the Sullivan boys were nice guys, but they were known to be a bit on the wild side themselves.

Sharon looked as if she was going to argue, then thought better of it.

"I know. But I've known them since they were kids. I'm sure I can rely on them."

Tom and Mary each agreed that the Sullivans could be trusted to stay in the Peabody Mansion, yet it seemed unlikely those two would be the ones to crack the case.

"So, does Sheriff Wilks think the house robberies and the pickpocketing are related?" Mary moved the plate of pumpkin bread to Tom, who still just sipped his coffee.

"He's not sure," Tom replied as he held up his hand to decline the bread. "I'm sorry, I'm not a big fan of pumpkin."

"You have to taste it before you say that!" Sharon was not going to let this opportunity slip by. "Plus, you're the perfect taste tester. If this bread can win you over, then Mary's trophy is practically in the bag."

The award for winning the baking contest wasn't actually a trophy, Mary mused to herself. It was a Christmas ornament with the winner's name and the year, so 'on the tree' was more accurate, really.

"And, you owe me for outing my secret," Mary added, giving Tom a pointed look.

Tom's brow creased in genuine confusion. "What secret?"

"You outed that she's a psychic to her crush," Sharon stated flatly before biting into her second slice.

Mary grimaced. Did all her secrets need to be revealed in one night?

"Oh," Tom said with a dawning understanding. "I thought Nathan was already your beau."

"Right?" Sharon almost choked.

"Well, he's not," Mary sounded more annoyed than she intended. But that was because she'd barely caught herself before she asked, 'Do you really think he likes me?' like a boy-crazy teenager. She needed to get a grip.

"I'm sorry about that," Tom said honestly. "Although if I had your abilities, I'd flaunt them."

"Right?" Sharon called out, this time with a teenager's inflection. Soon Sharon would be responding with comments like Mary's pumpkin bread was dope and she'd start calling Nathan Mary's babe.

"Well, he isn't. And I prefer to keep my intuition private."

"Intuition." Sharon actually gave her a reproving look. "You have your Aunt Bridget's abilities. You should be proud of that."

Mary had adored her Aunt Bridget, but she wasn't sure she had the same gumption that her feisty aunt had. Aunt Bridget never cared if people thought she was a little eccentric. She had worn her psychic ability like a badge of honor. Maybe Mary needed to do the same thing. But it was hard. She didn't feel she could do that quite yet.

Tom must have seen Mary's indecision, because he immediately surprised her by taking a piece of the pumpkin bread.

"It's the least I can do to make it up to you," he told her. "I would never want to do anything to make you feel uncomfortable."

"You don't really have to try it," Mary responded. Heaven knew, if someone forced her to eat fruit cake—no matter how good they told her it was —she would have been miserable.

"Well," he said, eyeing the spicy bread dubiously, "if I give it a thumbs up, then you know you've got a winner."

He took a bite, chewed a bit, and then gave her a wide-eyed look. "This is actually really good."

His reaction wasn't nearly as gushing as Sharon's, but Mary would take it, and to her surprise, he finished the whole piece.

Sharon hid a yawn behind her hand. "Okay, I've had my cocktail and my dinner, I think I am going to head home. I didn't get much sleep last night. I hope tonight is more restful."

Tom polished off the remainder of his coffee and stood up, too. "I need to get going as well. Thank you for the delicious coffee, Mary, and the piece of your winning bread."

Mary rose from the table to walk them out.

"I'll see you tomorrow at the parade," Sharon said after she had pulled on her coat and gave her friend a hug. "Hopefully I'll get to sleep in tomorrow. At least for a little while."

In truth, Mary was tired, too, and tomorrow was another busy day. The parade and then the

Christmas house tour. Fortunately, the house tour only ran for one night.

Sharon said her goodbyes and slipped out into the chilly night air.

"I wish that I'd had more information for you," Tom said as he put on his tweed cap.

"I wish I had more information for you, too."

Tom met her gaze, his blue eyes sincere. "Oh, I fully believe something will come to you."

He tipped his hat and then left the Inn.

Mary watched out the window to make sure that both of them made it to their cars and then she locked up her house.

When she turned away from the door she saw both her pets sitting in the foyer. They both waited patiently for their dinners.

Cindah meowed grumpily.

Okay, maybe not that patiently.

As she headed back to the kitchen and prepared her pets' suppers, she thought about Aunt Bridget and her open acceptance of her psychic abilities.

"How did you get so comfortable and confident with it?" Mary asked aloud.

"I just accepted it, Miss Sassypants." The voice in Mary's head responded so clearly that she stopped peeling the top off the cat food can in her hand and looked around.

"Aunt Bridget?"

Mary waited for a reply, but the house was silent, except for another impatient yowl from Cindah.

Mary shook her head, laughing at her own silliness.

She finished preparing Starlight and Cindah's bowls and placed them on the floor. Then she pulled out her phone and opened the app for her Christmas playlist. She turned on the Bluetooth speaker that she kept on the counter and pressed shuffle on the playlist.

Mary went to the fridge to find something for her own supper. Pumpkin bread wasn't going to cut it for her. The music started, and she froze.

Bing Crosby's distinct and mellow voice filled the room. But it wasn't one of his traditional Christmas songs. It was When Irish Eyes Are

Smiling. One of her Aunt Bridget's favorite songs.

Mary walked back to where she had placed her phone and picked it up. Instead of the Christmas playlist that she was sure she had tapped, another playlist was pulled up that she had titled, 'Aunt Bridget.'

Mary looked around the room again, then smiled.

CHAPTER 6

"I'm glad we got here early," Sharon said, looking around at the crowd-lined street. "We never would have gotten a decent spot if we had met at one like we originally planned."

Mary smiled at her friend. "I never knew you were so particular about event locations."

"If I'm going to stand out in the cold, then I'm going to make sure I at least get a good view," Sharon pointed out.

Mary looked up at the gray sky. The clouds and chilly air felt as if they could get some snow. Mary had been so busy with all of the Christmas hullabaloo; she hadn't even heard a weather report for days. But she did hope for just a little snow.

Someone bumped into her from behind, and Mary jumped, immediately thinking of a pickpocket. She whipped around only to find a little girl dancing with excitement for the parade to begin.

"Sorry," the little girl's clearly stressed mother apologized.

Mary smiled understandingly, her pulse calming to see it wasn't someone with dastardly intentions. Although the child did have a large, very sticky-looking, lollipop clutched in her small fist. But a sticky coat was better than thievery.

"Remember, Santa's watching." Sharon had leaned past Mary to say the admonition to the child, who instantly looked stricken.

The mother shot Sharon a dirty look and ushered her child away.

Mary chuckled softly despite herself. "That was not very Christmas-spirited of you."

"Hey, at least, I didn't mention that elf on the shelf thing. Now, that's creepy."

Mary supposed that was a small blessing. Elf on the shelf was creepy.

"Oh, I think I hear the marching bands getting ready," Sharon pushed slightly forward to peer past the line of people down the street.

Rather than focusing on the start of the parade, Mary scanned the crowd.

"Are you trying to see if you can spot the pickpocket?" Sharon asked.

"Yes," Mary said automatically.

Sharon gave her a knowing look. "Or are you looking for hottie-mctottie cheese man?"

Mary cast a look around them self-consciously. As if anybody would know who Sharon was referring to anyway. Although Mary wasn't sure there were that many cheese men on the Island. Especially, hottie-mctottie ones.

"No, I'm just looking at the crowd."

"Mm-hm."

Mary rolled her eyes at her friend, then someone tapped her on the shoulder. Again, she spun around slightly spooked, although hoping it was Nathan.

But this time, she was greeted by Angelica Moonshadow, Mary's eccentric New Age friend. She looked like a Christmas fairy in her white velvet cape that was embroidered with glittering silver threads with a white velvet beret to match. Her pretty face had turned rosy from the cold making her look downright elfin.

"Happy Yule!" Angelica said with an ethereal smile.

"Happy Yule," Mary replied back. She hadn't been sure if Angelica practiced Wicca, or some other unusual belief system, but her greeting basically confirmed her suspicions. Then she remembered Sharon beside her, watching them.

"I'm not sure if you have met my friend Sharon." Mary said to Angelica and was surprised when the two women smiled warmly at each other.

"Oh, Sharon and I have known each other for years."

Mary glanced back-and-forth between the two of them. "I had no idea you knew each other."

"I've been going to Angelica's shop since it opened," Sharon explained as if Mary should know that. And in truth, she probably should. It wasn't as if she and Sharon didn't hang out all the time.

"Yes, Angelica does readings for me," Sharon continued.

Mary gaped at her friend. "Readings?"

"I started going to Angelica after Bridget passed away. Your aunt used to do readings for me all the time."

Mary nodded. She guessed she should've realized that, too. Aunt Bridget loved to dabble with things like Tarot, Crystals and pendulums, so of course, she shared them with her best friend.

"It's funny that you should mention Bridget," Angelica said.

Mary now turned her surprised gaze on her New Age friend. "You knew my aunt?"

She shook her head with a genuine look of sorrow. "No, unfortunately, she passed before I moved here. But Sharon has told me a lot about her. She was clearly a very talented seer. I actually have a little something for both of you. From her."

Mary was thoroughly confused. The crowd around them began to cheer as the parade started, but she was barely aware of it.

Angelica pulled out two small rectangular boxes from a pocket buried in the folds of her cape. The boxes were tied with a simple red bow. She handed one to each of them.

Both women untied the boxes and peeked inside.

As soon as Mary saw what was nestled in the jewelry batten she felt a wave of warmth like arms hugging her. A beautiful silver necklace with a Celtic knot pendant glistened up at her.

"I got a shipment of jewelry in the shop for the holiday season, and as soon as I saw these two pendants, I just had the strong feeling that they were meant for both of you." Angelica smiled sweetly.

Mary couldn't speak. She stared at the charm, the exact charm that her Aunt Bridget always wore on a bracelet. A bracelet that she had left to Mary. A bracelet that she had on right now.

"This is beautiful!" Sharon exclaimed, holding up the necklace in her box-- also a Celtic knot. But not the same style as Mary's.

Finally, Mary met Angelica's gaze. "This is exactly the same charm my aunt always wore. How did you know?"

"She told me," Angelica said simply.

Still stunned, Mary didn't know what else to say but thank you.

Angelica gave Mary a quick hug and then gestured toward the street. "The parade is coming. You don't want to miss it. I just wanted to make sure you got those, but now I need to head back to my shop. This is a busy time of year for me."

Both Sharon and Mary watched as Angelica flitted into the crowd like a shimmering white angel.

"See," Sharon said, "people really do have special abilities. Including you."

Mary still stared at the necklace cupped in her hand, even as the first of the spectacular Christmas floats rolled past them.

It wasn't until she heard a snarky voice beside her that she snapped out of her amazed reverie.

"That woman is so strange."

Mary didn't even have to look to know who was standing next to her. She could recognize Yammering Yvonne's voice anywhere. Yvonne Luce had a voice like fingernails on a chalkboard.

Sharon didn't contain her annoyed groan, obviously hearing her, too. The Gossip Gang was here to ruin a perfectly magical Christmas moment.

"I heard that she's a witch or something," Yvonne's ever-present sidekick, Gail—or as Sharon liked to call her, Gossiping Gail—muttered.

The third of Yvonne's little group of gossips, Whispering Winnie Mayhew piped in something, but Mary couldn't hear her usual, meek tone over the horns of the marching band moving past them in perfect lockstep.

"Just ignore them," Mary leaned in to tell Sharon. "They love it when people respond to their nonsense."

"I'd like to respond by popping Yvonne right in her yammering mouth," Sharon sputtered, but she kept her gaze on the stunning float covered in red and white poinsettias that rolled by.

Sharon and Yvonne had been adversaries since their high school days. Frankly, Mary was shocked that the two of them hadn't come to blows long ago. Or maybe they had. Mary was starting to realize that she didn't know everything about her bestie.

Although the Gossip Gang remained beside them, fortunately the two friends couldn't hear anything else they were saying over the cheers and music of the parade.

In fact, both Mary and Sharon were soon distracted by the sights and the energy of the crowd around them. They got to see Santa and his elves. Alpacas wearing felt reindeer antlers on their woolly heads. Even the Grinch made an appearance, to the vocal joy of children all around them.

And the most fortunate thing of all was that when the parade was over and the people started to disperse, the Gossip Gang left, too!

"I wonder why Nathan didn't show up?" Mary asked her friend trying to sound more curious than disappointed.

"He probably saw the Gossip Gang and hid," Sharon answered, as she stepped out into the still-closed-off street.

"I'm proud of you, though. You made it through it without any bloodshed." Mary grinned.

No sooner had she said that, someone bumped into Sharon, hard, practically knocking the older woman off her feet.

Mary's heart raced as she reached out to steady Sharon. "Are you okay?"

Sharon nodded, looking around to see who had slammed into her.

They both spotted a slight person, in a black hoodie, dodging through the crowd, knocking into a few other people, but quickly disappearing into the morass of confused onlookers.

"That was the pickpocket," Mary said with certainty.

"Hey!" a male voice called, and they both turned to see Nathan. He rushed toward them, his gaze moving over them with concern. "Are you two all right? I saw what happened."

Sharon pulled in a deep breath. "I'm fine. More startled than anything."

"Are you sure the guy didn't steal anything?" Mary asked.

"I didn't bring a purse today for this very reason."

"Well, they're called pickpockets for a reason," Mary pointed out. "You better check your pockets to see that you have everything."

Mary and Nathan moved to either side of the older woman and led her over to a storefront in order to get her out of the line of foot traffic.

"I have my wallet and the necklace Angelica gave me," Sharon said as she pulled the items out of the large pockets of her winter coat to show them. "I have my cell phone, too. Keys. It looks like I have everything." Then she paused and checked all her pockets again. She groaned. "My keys to the mansion. I had them on a separate key ring. They're gone!"

"We better head over to the Peabody Mansion right now to check things out!" Mary suggested.

"But how would they know where I live, or what the keys are for?" Sharon asked. "I think that person just reached in my pocket and grabbed the first thing he touched."

That was a valid point, but Mary's brain was humming like an oscillating fan on high telling her something was amiss.

Sharon wiped her hand over her brow, the movement agitated. "I don't have time for this nonsense right now. Not with the house tour tonight."

Mary knew her friend was probably right. Pickpocketing was a crime of opportunity. But still, Mary knew something wasn't right with this robbery.

"At least, let us go over with you to the mansion and make sure everything's okay there. I know you have a lot to do, so I can contact Tom. I think he at least should know what happened."

"I think that's a good idea, too," Nathan offered. "Do you have another set of keys to the mansion?"

Sharon sighed. "Not on me but the Sullivan brothers are there. So they can let us in."

That was good news, at least.

Mary put her hand around Sharon's shoulder. "Okay, so why don't we head over there? I think it would still be wise to try to get a locksmith over to change the locks, too. It can't hurt anyway. And I'll just call Tom and let him know about the pickpocket. I know we don't have much to go on, but I think he should know. Then he can contact Sheriff Wilks."

"Yes, that would be good," Sharon agreed, still looking frazzled. This was truly the last thing she needed on her mind.

"Great, we have a plan." Nathan said as he put a comforting hand on Sharon's other shoulder.

"You don't have to go with us," Mary said. "I'm sure you have other things you need to do."

"No, not a thing to do other than help you wonderful women."

***

"You have got to be kidding," Sharon stammered as she knocked on the front door of her mansion for the third time. "Where are they?"

Just as she was about to knock for the fourth time with some frustrated gusto, the door finally opened. Sharon nearly clocked Doug Sullivan in the jaw, who was standing in front of her, blinking and yawning.

"Sorry about that," the barrel-chested man in his mid-twenties said, running a hand through his thick red hair, so that the mussed locks stood up on his head like a rooster comb. "I must've dozed off."

Sharon pushed past the groggy man to enter the house. "Where's Kevin?"

Doug blinked. "I think he had to help Mom set up the Christmas tree. I did it last year."

Sharon frowned at him. "I hired both of you to watch the mansion, and you're asleep, and your brother is gone."

"I'm sorry." Doug had the good grace to look embarrassed.

"But you know how mom is when she wants something done. And I didn't mean to fall asleep, but it's kind of— quiet around here. I mean, there isn't even cable. I guess I just sort of fell asleep."

"I wish it was sort of quiet around here," Sharon grumbled as she headed for the kitchen.

Mary started to follow her friend, but Nathan's hand on her arm made her stop.

"I'm going to ask Doug to check around the mansion. Just to make sure everything looks okay." Nathan said as he looked at Mary with genuine concern.

Mary nodded. "That would be great. I'm just going to check on Sharon and then I'll give Tom a call."

Mary heard Nathan call to Doug as she headed to the kitchen, and from Doug's hoarse reply, it sounded as if he'd already dozed off again. Tom had clearly been right about the Sullivan brothers. Not the sharpest tools in the shed.

As expected, Mary was greeted by the rattle of ice in a shaker. Sharon looked up guiltily when she heard her enter the room.

"I know it's a bit early for a cocktail, but this has been a doozy of a Christmas season."

"No judgment from me," Mary assured her. If Sharon had any wine she might have had a glass herself. She took a seat at the kitchen island. "Nathan and Doug are taking a look around the house just to make sure nothing looks unusual."

Looking less stressed, yet more depressed, Sharon began sipping her martini. "None of this is going how I imagined. I wanted this to be a real sendoff for the mansion. And for Edwin."

Mary reached out to hold her friend's hand. "It will be. I'm sure you're right about the pickpocket. He probably just snatched whatever he could reach. But I still think it's wise to be cautious."

Sharon agreed again. "I know you're right." Then she lifted her martini glass again. "And this will help."

Mary smiled indulgently at her friend as she watched her take a drink. After sitting with Sharon for a while longer, she excused herself to call Tom.

She called him at the station, assuming he was probably at work. He answered on the first ring. "Constable Andrews."

"Hi, Tom. It's Mary."

"I was expecting your call."

"You were?"

"Yes, I heard from Sheriff Wilks that the pickpocket was busy at the parade. And I knew you and Sharon were going to be there."

"Yes, Sharon was one of the people who got hit."

"Really?" His tone was a combination of disbelief and sympathy. "She is really having a rough couple of days. Is she okay? Did you see the person?"

"She's fine. Stressed but not hurt. And we only really got a look at him when he was already fleeing the scene. I just saw someone in a black hoodie. I'm not even sure if it was a man or a woman."

"Yeah, it seems as though whoever is doing this is pretty good at it. Sheriff Wilk said that everybody seems to be giving different descriptions. But that's common with witnesses who are high or intoxicated. They're notoriously unreliable. What did he steal from Sharon?"

"All the thief got was the keys to the Peabody Mansion."

Tom was silent for a moment. "And you're thinking that was exactly what they were trying to get?"

"That's my worry. But I don't know for sure."

Tom was quiet again, then said, "I'll plan to be at Sharon's house tonight."

"I think that would make Sharon feel better, that's for sure."

"Then I'll see you there."

"Thanks, Tom."

Mary hung up the phone, already feeling a lot better. She knew that Sharon would feel much more relaxed knowing that Tom would be here.

They would help her get through this night without a hitch, and then they could worry about changing the locks and ramping up the security system.

It was just one night.

CHAPTER 7

Shortly after Mary was done talking to Tom, Nathan returned. Sharon was on the phone with a locksmith, trying to arrange for somebody to come tomorrow to replace the locks.

Nathan stopped in the kitchen doorway and waved for Mary to come with him. Clearly, he wanted to tell her something that he didn't want Sharon to know.

"Did you find something?" Mary asked as soon as they were in the dining room and out of earshot from Sharon.

"Everything looked fine, except there was a window open to the cellar. It's a small window that I don't think anyone could get through. Certainly not an adult. And it doesn't look as if the ground around the window was disturbed. But it's kind of hard to tell with the ground being frozen. Doug and I went down into the basement to look around, too. Nothing seems disturbed down there either. Who knows, maybe it's been open for a while."

Mary glanced back toward the kitchen. She could still hear Sharon on the phone.

"Did you notice anything else?"

"I'm sure this doesn't tie-in, but Doug and I heard an argument from the house next door. Neither of us could make out what was being said, but the voices seemed to be male."

"Which house?"

Nathan pointed to the dining room window. "The one over there."

The Vanderhoops.

"Oh, and Kevin is back, too. I told both brothers how important it is for them to stay in the house. And to keep double checking things. Just in case."

Mary nodded, appreciating Nathan's help. "I think the best bet right now is to just get through this night. Maybe we should mention the window to Tom, but I don't think we should say anything to Sharon."

"Say what to Sharon?" Sharon appeared in the doorway, giving them a curious look.

Mary froze, surprised Sharon was off the phone, and unsure of what to say.

"That I asked Mary out to dinner," Nathan said, managing a very believably sheepish look.

Sharon frowned at Mary. "Why wouldn't you want me to know that Nathan asked you out for dinner?"

Nathan sighed. "Maybe she was planning to reject my invitation."

Sharon looked confused at Mary. "Why would you reject his invitation? You've been wanting to go on a date with Nathan for months."

Mary fought the urge to close her eyes and groan. Seriously? Her friends were killing her here.

"Well? Are you going to go out or what?" Sharon blurted out after a moment. She widened her eyes as if to silently tell her she would be insane if she said no.

Except, again, this was a completely fictional conversation. From start to finish—well except for the part where she had been hoping Nathan would ask her out. Could the floor open up and swallow her whole? Please.

"Yes, Mary, would you go out to dinner with me?" Nathan asked.

Mary looked back and forth between the two of them, then said, "Yes!"

Sharon clapped her hands excitedly. The next thing Mary knew her friend was ushering the two of them toward the front door. "Why don't you go get dinner now?"

Mary stopped in the foyer and said "Sharon, I don't want to leave you right now. I know you have things you need to get done before the tour. I want to stay and help you."

Sharon made a dismissive snort and waved her hand. "You two have plenty of time to have a nice early dinner." Then she glanced at where the Sullivan brothers lounged in the front living room. Both of them looked like frat boys at their fraternity house rather than security. "Plus, I have those two here, and I need to put them to work anyway."

Mary looked at Nathan helplessly. He shrugged as if he had no idea what to say.

"Go," Sharon insisted, pointing at the front door. "It's Christmas time. Go have some fun. I'll be totally fine here."

Mary reluctantly nodded. "Okay, but I will be back in plenty of time for the tour."

Sharon smiled, and Mary realized this was the first time that she had looked genuinely happy for the past couple of days. Too bad it was a fake date that had finally cheered her up.

Mary grabbed her coat and followed Nathan outside.

"Have fun and don't worry about me." Sharon beamed and waved to them. Mary was relieved, at least to hear her lock the door after them.

Once on the sidewalk Nathan and Mary looked at each other awkwardly.

"I'm sorry about that," Nathan said. "I guess I just sort of panicked when I saw Sharon and said the first thing that came into my head."

"That's okay. I'm sorry that Sharon made that comment about me wanting to go to dinner with you for months."

Nathan made a face, looking wounded. "You haven't wanted to go out with me?"

Mary glanced around the street. A few people were bustling down the sidewalk with bags from local shops. They chatted and laughed easily with Christmas cheer, and she wondered how she got into this strange, uneasy situation.

"Because I've been wanting to ask you out on a date for months myself."

Mary blinked at Nathan; not quite sure she had heard him correctly. Everything was so surreal; it was just as likely that she had imagined his comment.

Finally, she found her voice. "You have?"

He grinned a little sheepishly. "That's why it was the first thing to pop out of my mouth when I saw Sharon. I've been wanting to ask you out since our dance at Janis' get together."

"So, how come you didn't?" Mary asked, stunned but also very curious.

Nathan shoved his hands in the pocket of his peacoat. "I guess I was intimidated."

Mary gaped at him. "By me? Why?"

"Well, you're smart and beautiful. You were a high-powered lawyer and now a successful business owner, and I'm the cheese guy."

Hottie McTottie cheese guy plus he was a writer, Mary thought, still not totally processing what was happening.

"Well, um, thank you, Nathan. And our age difference doesn't bother you?" Mary was suddenly acutely aware of being about ten years older than this gorgeous man.

Nathan looked confused. "That is the one thing that doesn't give me hesitation."

They both stood there as if not sure what to say.

Then finally, Nathan spoke up. "Mary Hogan, would you like to go out to dinner with me?"

Mary nodded. "Yes, I'd love to."

They fell into step with each other, not touching, but walking in a happy silence.

That was until the door to the Vanderhoops flew open and a young man with shaggy, disheveled hair fled out. He jumped down the front steps, his escape followed by the loud, angry shouts of another male voice from inside.

The other man, who was still yelling, appeared in the open doorway.

"Get back here," he snarled after the boy.

Mary immediately recognized the man in the door as the one who had spoken to them the night of the attempted break-in at Sharon's. "The Nephew."

The boy didn't slow down. He tugged up the gray hood to his sweatshirt and kept running down the sidewalk ahead of them. Something about his movements and his physique was familiar to Mary.

The man in the doorway noticed Mary and Nathan staring at him. He scowled in their direction and then slammed the door shut.

"What was that all about?" Nathan asked, still watching the boy race down the street. The kid turned the corner and disappeared down one of the side roads.

Mary shook her head. "I have no idea. But there's definitely something very wrong at that place."

They started walking, heading to Edgartown's Main Street.

"This has been a strange Christmas season," Nathan agreed.

They both fell silent. Mary tried to lose herself in admiring all of the old homes with their Greek Revival architecture. Huge white houses perfectly maintained to display their stately magnificence. But her thoughts kept going back to that neighbor and the boy running away from him. What was going on over at the Vanderhoops? The police said that the man was there with his kids. Were those kids safe?

"Do you like tapas?" Nathan asked as they reached Main Street. He pointed to a building with a bright red and white awning.

"Oh, is this Isabella's? I read about it opening in the Vineyard Gazette. I have been wanting to try it," Mary said.

Nathan looked pleased. "I've been wanting to try it, too."

Isabella's was not a large place, but the ambience was warm and welcoming. With white covered tables with candles and holly in the center. Mary was surprised to see that the place wasn't busier. But it was still early.

"Hey, I might be able to get us the senior early bird special," Mary teased.

Instead of laughing, Nathan regarded her seriously. "Does our age difference really bother you? Because quite honestly I don't think there's a person here who would even know there's any age difference."

Mary considered the question. Honestly, if it didn't bother him, she didn't see a reason it should bother her. It wasn't as if she was an old lady. And forties were the new thirties now anyway, right?

Finally, she took a few deep breaths. "No, it doesn't bother me." Not that much anyway, but she didn't say that aloud.

Instead, she gave him a conspiratorial look. "But I do have something I have to admit."

Nathan tilted his head, eyeing her curiously. "Oh yeah, what's that?"

"I'm not actually old enough to get any senior discounts."

Nathan laughed. "Darn it. I thought that was going to be a perk of dating you."

She smiled, taking note that he said dating. Like this wasn't a onetime deal.

Just then, a hostess approached them with menus in hand.

"Table for two?" she asked with a friendly smile. Mary noticed that she had on Santa hat earrings. Cute.

"Yes," Nathan said.

The young lady led them to a table near a small Christmas tree that was lit with multicolored lights.

After they were seated, the hostess handed them their menus. "Can I put in your drink order while you wait for your server?"

Nathan looked to Mary for her answer.

"I'll have a glass of Sauvignon Blanc." Mary hoped the glass of wine would temper some of the nervous energy, that was still making her a little tense.

Nathan perused the beer list, then said, "I'll try the Krampus stout."

The hostess nodded and headed toward the small bar set up near the doorway to the kitchen.

"Krampus?" Mary said, "I'm not sure we should risk inviting him into this holiday season."

"Yeah, you're probably right. Although I think things will have to calm down here soon, right?"

Mary wanted to agree with him, but she still had a strange feeling that she just couldn't shake.

He studied her for a moment. "So, is what Tom said about you true?"

Mary should've guessed that he was going to ask about that. And frankly, it was out there now.

Plus, between the strange feelings inside herself for the past couple days, as well as the experiences related to Aunt Bridget, maybe it was time to be a little more open. She got the feeling that was what Aunt Bridget was trying to tell her.

"I do have some abilities, which I think I got from my aunt. She believed it runs in our family. But it isn't like you see on TV or in movies."

She waited for Nathan's doubtful reaction. But instead, he just nodded, listening.

"Do you…" before she could finish, asking her question, their server, a man in his twenties, tall and wiry, approached the table to deliver their drinks.

Mary looked at the man and at that very moment, her brain started buzzing again. She knew she'd never seen this young man before, but he reminded her of someone.

"Did you need a moment to look at the menu?" he asked, clearly confused by Mary's dazed look.

"Yes," she managed.

As soon as the waiter left the table, Nathan leaned forward to ask quietly, "Are you okay?"

Mary blinked at him. "That man looks like someone I've recently met. Not him specifically, but someone."

"Is this part of your abilities?"

Mary couldn't believe how readily Nathan was accepting that she may be psychic. No, scratch that. That she was psychic.

"Yes, I think so. But the most frustrating part of my abilities is sometimes it's very clear. And other times, like now, it's just this sort of weird inkling that I should be putting something together that I'm not."

"Maybe it's like a lot of things in life, maybe when you're too close to it or thinking about it too hard, you can't see it. Maybe you just need to distance yourself and relax."

Mary stared at him. Hottie-McTottie cheese man was not only handsome but wise, too.

She took a sip of her wine. He was right. She needed to give herself a break, and simply enjoy their dinner together.

"Well, that definitely lived up to the good reviews," Mary said as they both got ready to head back to the Peabody Mansion.

"I loved those fried goat cheese things," Nathan concurred, then gave her a lopsided smile as he helped her put on her coat. "Although I think my goat cheese is a little bit better."

"You should contact them about buying their cheese through you."

"Oh, I plan to."

Mary thanked him for the help with her coat and then they both headed to the door.

"Look," Mary breathed as they got to the door.

The two of them had been so wrapped up in their conversation and the delicious food that they hadn't even noticed that fluffy white snowflakes had started to fall.

"I heard on the radio we were supposed to get snow tonight," Nathan said, stepping out into the flakes. "Nothing major, just a dusting."

"Perfect." Mary smiled at the beauty of it. "Just enough to make it feel Christmasy."

She pulled back the sleeve of her coat to check her watch. "Oh gosh, we were there longer than I thought we would be. I guess we better head back and see if Sharon needs any help with anything."

They hurried back to the Peabody Mansion, although Mary would have liked to have taken more time and enjoyed the gently falling snow and the twinkling of Christmas lights on all the houses. And Nathan's company, most of all.

When they arrived at the mansion, they saw a ladder leaning up against the front porch. Both Sullivan brothers were up on the roof, arguing.

"No, it's not that bulb. We already tested that one," Doug said impatiently.

Kevin scowled at his brother. "No, we tested the one next to it."

Doug nudged his brother out of the way. "Just let me do it."

If those two weren't careful, one of them was going to fall off the roof.

"Everything okay up there?" Nathan called up to them.

Both brothers turned, clearly startled, as if Nathan's voice had come to them out of the ethers Finally, they spotted Nathan and Mary on the walkway. Looking up at them.

"The Christmas lights just went out. They were working fine half an hour ago. We're trying to get them fixed before the tours start to arrive," Doug explained.

Mary had her doubts that they'd figure out the problem before then. Not if they kept arguing with each other.

"I think I better go up and try to help them," Nathan suggested, giving Mary a wry look.

Mary laughed softly, looked up at the two brothers, then back at Nathan.

"I think you're right." She laughed softly and shook her head. "I'm going to go inside and see if I can help Sharon."

"I hope things are going better in there," Nathan said, looking back up to the brothers, who were again bickering.

Mary turned back to look at Nathan one more time before she headed up the steps. All they had to do was get through tonight's tour. It started at seven, and the last tour came through at ten. So, three to four hours. Surely, they could make it through that.

Mary scraped her shoes off on the doormat and tried the door. Of course, it was unlocked. Which shouldn't be such a big deal, since the Sullivan brothers were outside. But she suspected a group of marauding pirates could have entered the Peabody Mansion and those two would have never noticed.

The scene inside of the house was much nicer than the one outside. Christmas music drifted through the air, intermingled with the aroma of vanilla and spice. From the direction of the kitchen, she could hear Sharon talking to someone.

Mary started toward the back of the house. She was greeted by Sharon, filling a large carafe with a spigot full of coffee. She had also set out paper coffee cups along with cartons of creamer and packets of sugar. And there were several platters of cookies.

"When did you do all this?" Mary asked, impressed. Sharon was not the type to bake cookies.

Sharon grinned at her. "Instacart is an amazing thing."

Mary laughed, still impressed. "But it even smells like you've been baking."

Sharon pointed to a wax warmer in the shape of a snowman on the counter. Wax melted in the top of his hat. Then she put a finger to her lips. "But that will be our little secret."

"Very sneaky," Mary whispered.

"I'm not doing this," a voice called out from the hallway that led upstairs.

"Is that Tom?" Mary was pretty sure she recognized the muffled voice. Why was his voice muffled, anyway?

Sharon grinned, and Mary couldn't miss the impish look on her face.

A few moments later Tom entered the kitchen. Or at least Mary thought it was Tom.

"Santa!" she exclaimed, trying not to laugh.

Tom stood in the doorway in a full red and white suit. The white beard disguised most of his face, but Mary could still tell it was him from his piercing blue eyes, which looked utterly miserable.

"Tom graciously agreed to play Santa tonight," Sharon explained, quite pleased with herself.

"Tom did not agree," he muttered. "Tom was harangued into it."

Sharon feigned an offended look. "I have never harangued anybody in my whole life."

Knowing that was far from the truth, Mary and Tom exchanged a look. Sharon could be relentless when she wanted something. And apparently, she wanted a Santa for tonight's event.

"Well, I think you look fantastic," Mary assured him.

Tom didn't look as if he believed her for one moment. In truth, he was kind of a bedraggled-looking Santa--which was not trendy for his style. But Mary had no doubt that the children on the tour would be thrilled at his presence.

"Okay," Nathan strode into the room. "The Christmas lights are up and all lit" His gaze landed on Tom, but he was not as successful at keeping his amusement in check as Mary and Sharon had been.

He laughed heartily, and Mary thought again, not for the first time tonight, that Nathan had the best laugh. Deep and genuine.

"Why, hello, Santa. I didn't expect to see you here tonight," Nathan chuckled.

"I didn't expect to be here tonight," Tom retorted dryly.

Nathan laughed again.

Sharon finished setting up the refreshments on the island, then looked at the clock on the double ovens. "All right, I think everything is done, and we even have time to spare."

"Where do you want us be stationed?" Mary asked. She and Sharon had already discussed that it would probably be best to have them situated around the house to keep the tour organized and moving.

"Well," Sharon began, "I'm going to be in the front room with the Christmas tree. Nathan, if you don't mind being in the dining room to sort of direct traffic. Mary, I'm going to let you man the refreshment station. And Tom—or, rather Santa—you should obviously greet the people as they come in."

"Great," Tom mumbled as he schlepped out of the kitchen and toward the front door. Edwin apparently had bigger feet than Tom.

Mary, Nathan, and Sharon exchanged amused looks and more laughter filled the kitchen.

"I can hear you!" Tom called back to them. "You're all on Santa's naughty list."

The three of them laughed even harder.

"I'll go get him a position, too," Nathan added, still grinning as he left the room.

"It looks like everything has come together pretty well," Mary said reassuringly, moving to stand behind the island.

Sharon gave her friend a wide smile. "Other than the near disaster with the outside lights. And a run-in with that guy staying at the Vanderhoops."

Mary frowned, immediately concerned. "What happened?"

"I went over there to see if they had a ladder that we could borrow. I guess I must've taken the one we had here back to my place. Anyway, when I went over there and knocked on the door there was clearly some sort of ruckus going on inside. And when that strange guy answered the door, he was incredibly rude. The Vandehoops are rude, but not that kind of rude. That guy is a real creep."

Mary nodded. She agreed one hundred percent.

"Fortunately, Doug and Kevin ran home to get one from their house."

Mary wasn't thrilled that Sharon had been here by herself, even for a little while. But it seemed as if everything had gone fine.

Just then, the front doorbell rang, which was followed by Tom's surprisingly inspired deep, "Ho, ho, ho."

Sharon made an impressed face. "See, I knew he was the right one for the job."

She grinned proudly and headed toward the living room to greet her visitors.

Mary smiled to herself, too. She really hoped that none of Tom's police buddies were on the tour tonight. He'd never live this down.

CHAPTER 8

The tour was going amazingly well. Everyone was oohing and ahhing over Sharon's glorious home. She had really pulled it off. The decorations were amazing. People were enjoying the snacks. Overall, Mary couldn't imagine things going any better.

That was until she heard a gratingly familiar voice.

"I suppose some people like this sort of thing. All these old ornaments. I personally find them a bit garish."

Great, Mary thought. Yammering Yvonne and her cronies. Of course, they would have to make an appearance.

Sure enough, the three women strolled into the kitchen.

"Oh, look, refreshments," Gossiping Gail said, and for a moment, Mary thought the comment was given with genuine appreciation. But then the short brunette added, "Of course they're store-bought, but I guess it's better than nothing."

Yvonne laughed, the sound more of a cackle. "Everyone knows that Sharon can't cook. That's why she's always had to marry rich. So her husbands," she emphasized the plural, "can hire people to do that for her."

"Mary," Whispering Winnie said. The meek woman always spoke as if she were about to share some particularly juicy tidbit of gossip. "I can't believe Sharon didn't wrangle you into baking for her."

Mary smiled sweetly. "I would've happily done it for her. But she knows how busy everyone is at this time of year."

"I love to take the time to bake for my family," Yvonne said as if she deserved an award for it.

Mary turned her unwaveringly kind smile on the woman. "Well, you aren't her family. And I think it was more than generous that she opened her home to everyone tonight. Have you considered having your home included in the tour?"

Yvonne lived in a condo, and no one wanted to tour that.

Yvonne's smug expression wavered for a moment. Then she rallied, again managing to look down her nose at Mary, even though Mary was several inches taller than the bottle blonde.

"Is there a restroom I could use?" Yvonne asked. "The Hillmen's offered a delicious, mulled cider, and I fear that I partook a little too much."

She cast a disparaging look at the mere offering of coffee that Sharon had available.

Mary had no doubt that she wanted to use Sharon's bathroom just so she could then criticize the cleanliness of it or something. Not that anyone would listen to her catty critique anyway.

Mary pointed toward the short hallway that led to the laundry room and bathroom.

Gail and Winnie eyed the selection of cookies as if Sharon had set out platters of liver and onions. Although those little vampires probably would have preferred meat. Rare.

A piercing scream filled the kitchen. All the joyous chatter of the other tour guests, who just entered the kitchen, fell silent.

Mary immediately headed toward the direction of the scream. It had come from the bathroom. But before she could enter the hallway, Yvonne staggered backwards into the kitchen. Her pinched face had turned a ghastly white.

Having heard the piercing shriek, Nathan pushed past the tour guests. He rushed to the stricken woman and helped her get to one of the kitchen stools.

Mary moved to the hallway to see what had upset her so badly. She didn't even need to enter the hallway to see what it was.

The bathroom door was wide open, an overhead light illuminating the small room. And there, on the white tiles of the bathroom floor, was a man slumped in an awkward position between the pedestal sink and the wall. And even from a distance, Mary could see he was badly hurt-- maybe even dead. But even through the bruises on his face, she recognized him. It was the same young man who had posed as a police officer.

She pulled in a steadying breath and returned to the kitchen. Trying to keep her expression calm, Mary said, "Nathan, go get Tom."

She then turned to a group of ten or fifteen guests, keeping her tone even and polite. "I'm sorry, folks, but we are going to have to cut the tour short this evening. There has been an accident, and we need to get some help here. Can I please have everyone just turn around and head calmly back toward the front door."

Thankfully, the guests did as she requested, muttering with disappointment and confusion, but ultimately exiting the mansion.

She passed Nathan and Tom as they hurried back toward the kitchen. Neither of the men stopped to ask her what had happened: they just rushed back in the direction of the bathroom.

Sharon came out of the sitting room when she saw Mary directing people outside. "What's going on?"

Mary managed a calm smile for the benefit of the guests. "Just a little accident in the bathroom. Tom and Nathan are handling it. But I think we're going to have to cut short the tour."

Sharon looked confused, but nevertheless nodded and started to help direct people back out to the street.

"Are Kevin and Doug still here?" Mary asked.

Sharon nodded.

"I think you better have them go out on the porch and tell people that the Peabody Mansion is closed for the evening."

Sharon gaped at Mary. "The accident is that bad?"

Mary bobbed her head solemnly. "Oh yeah."

Clearing the mansion went smoothly, and the Sullivan brothers had done a good job of making sure the tour moved past the Peabody Mansion and onto the next home.

Unfortunately, given the fact there was a half-dead stranger in Sharon's guest bath, there was no way to avoid the flashing lights of the police cars and ambulances that now lined the street in front of the mansion.

Sheriff Wilks, a bald and portly man, strode into the sitting room where Mary, Sharon, and Nathan sat, all of them looking dazed.

"Good evening," he greeted, his manner no nonsense. "I got a call from Constable Andrews. Is he still here?"

"Bob," Tom said as he walked into the sitting room, "you're going to want to come this way."

The sheriff's stoic look slipped slightly at the sight of Tom and his red suit.

At least Tom had thought of pulling off the hat and beard, Mary thought.

The two lawmen disappeared toward the bathroom.

"I don't understand," Sharon said. "I have no idea who that man is. Why would he be assaulted in my home?"

"And how did he even end up in the bathroom?" Nathan asked.

"The only time I wasn't in the house," Sharon said, "was when I went over to the Vanderhoop's house to try to borrow the ladder. I guess maybe Kevin and Doug could've been outside. But that couldn't have been more than, maybe, fifteen minutes. Otherwise, there was always somebody in the house. Not to mention, whoever brought that guy in here would've had to have brought him through the back door. Which has been locked the whole time."

"You didn't recognize him?" Mary seemed puzzled. "That was the young guy who was pretending to be a police officer."

Sharon's eyes widened. "You're right. That was him. But why put him in my bathroom?"

Mary agreed that none of this made any sense. She just hoped that Tom and Sheriff Wilks could see something that they hadn't seen.

They all fell silent, no one knowing what to say. This was crazy.

After a while, Sheriff Wilks and Tom returned to the living room.

"I'm going to have to ask all of you to come down to the Edgartown Police Station to give statements," the Sheriff said.

Mary wasn't exactly sure what their statements were supposed to be. They had no idea how the body got there, who the person was, or why he would be in Sharon's bathroom. None of it made sense.

"Can we just drive to the station?" Nathan asked.

Sheriff Wilks nodded. "Yeah, that's not a problem." He turned to Tom. "I'm going to have to stay here and try to see what evidence there is. If you want, you can go with your friends."

"Actually Bob, I'd like to stay here and see what you find out, too."

"I can drive Mary and Sharon to the station," Nathan offered.

"I think that's a good idea. And Kevin and Doug Sullivan will need to go give a statement as well. Not that I think those two knuckleheads saw anything," Tom said.

"Says the retired detective in a Santa suit," Sheriff Wilks pointed out.

Mary smiled, even though it seemed oddly inappropriate to be finding amusement now. She glanced at Sharon. Thankfully, her friend smiled slightly, too.

Mary felt bad, not only for the man who'd been assaulted but also for Sharon. This was supposed to be her small tribute to Edwin and his love of Christmas and his love of this house. This was not what she wanted Sharon's last memory of the place to be.

Nathan stood from where he sat beside Mary. "Should we go down to the station and get this over with?"

Both women nodded.

When they stepped out onto the street, Mary was dismayed to find a crowd of people still standing around, watching the spectacle going on. The snow was still falling, and they looked a bit like a warped nativity scene, grouped together on the sidewalk.

Nathan ushered them over to Mary's catering van that was parked in Sharon's driveway. Great, yet again her catering company was going to be directly linked to a murder.

"Do you want me to drive?" Nathan asked as he looked at Mary.

"Do you mind?" Mary replied. She could drive if she had to, but she had to admit that her brain was buzzing so loudly that it would definitely distract her on the road.

"Of course not," he said, offering her a reassuring smile.

Mary handed him her keys. She hated that he was going to be associated with this mess, too, but she was glad he was there.

She glanced at Sharon. Her friend looked shaken and practically dead on her feet. Again, probably not the best description.

Thankfully they didn't have to spend too long at the police station, and the female officer who took their statements was friendly and efficient. Soon, they were driving Nathan back to his car which was still parked near the parade route.

Did the parade really happen today? Mary wondered. It seemed like days ago now.

"Are you sure you two are going to be all right?" Nathan asked as he parked the van behind his truck. "I can stick around."

"I appreciate that," Mary said sincerely. "But I know you must be as tired as we are."

"Yes," Sharon added, smiling gratefully at him. "You've been a huge help. I'm pretty sure this was not how you thought your day would go."

He made an almost comical face. "No, I don't think I could've predicted any of this. But I'm still glad that I was here."

Both he and Mary got out of the van. She walked around to the driver's side.

"Are you really sure you're going to be okay?"

Mary gave Nathan's arm a slight squeeze. "I'm going to insist that Sharon stay at the inn with me tonight. And we will be fine."

To her surprise Nathan pulled her into a tight hug. Emotionally and physically exhausted, Mary gladly accepted it. His arms felt strong and reassuring around her, and until this moment, she hadn't realized how desperately she needed a hug.

"Even though this has been a truly insane night, scratch that whole day, I just want you to know our time together was the best time I've had in a long time," he said, his cheek resting on the top of her head.

She pulled back enough to look at his face. "Even hanging out at a police station?"

He laughed slightly. "Well, hopefully on our next date we can skip the police station and finding a beaten-up stranger in your friend's bathroom."

"Yeah, I would really like that."

For a moment Mary thought that Nathan was going to kiss her. But instead, he gave her another quick hug, then let her go. He waited until she was in the van and had the engine running, before heading to his own truck.

Sharon glanced at her. "Well, how was the date?"

Mary grinned back at her friend before putting the vehicle in to drive. "Is it weird after everything we've been through today to say it was pretty awesome?"

Sharon shook her head. "No, I think it's nice to hear that something good came out of this insane situation."

"Okay." Mary's tone turned serious. "I'm bringing you to the Inn and you are going to spend the night with me. No arguments."

Sharon dropped her head back onto the headrest of her seat and let her eyes drift shut. "I don't think I have the energy to argue. Not to mention, I don't think that I want to be alone tonight."

"Good," Mary felt extremely relieved that her often ornery friend was being amenable.

They were both silent for a moment.

"You know," Sharon blurted out, "I think the thing that bothers me the most about this whole crazy situation is the fact that that darned Yvonne Luce was the one to find the guy in my bathroom. That'll give her fodder to gossip about me for years to come."

Mary laughed, shaking her head. "I can see that. But at least we give her very good gossip."

Extremely tired, but genuinely amused, Sharon chuckled. "Never let it be said that we don't know how to make an impression."

CHAPTER 9

"No way. Absolutely not," Sharon said emphatically over her cup of morning coffee and slice of pumpkin bread. "You're not withdrawing from the baking competition."

Mary leaned on the counter, frowning at her friend. "It just doesn't seem appropriate after everything that happened last night."

Sharon made a face. "You didn't beat up that guy in the bathroom. Why should you lose your chance at Edgartown's champion baker award?"

"It's just a Christmas tree ornament, and there's always next year."

"Say that to the guy on my bathroom floor. That's a reminder not to put off the things that make you happy, if there ever was one," Sharon said dryly. "Plus, that ornament is coveted. I mean, how many people are entered into this competition?"

"I don't know, maybe thirty. Thirty-five."

"Well, this pumpkin bread is way better than thirty or thirty-five other peoples' baking on this island."

"I don't know," Mary repeated.

In her frustration, Sharon set her coffee down with more force than she intended. Startled by the loud noise, Starlight lifted her head from where she was sleeping on her dog bed. Cindah also woke up in the spot where she had been slumbering in the sunlight on the windowsill over the sink. With visible irritation at her sleep being disturbed, she blinked, rose, stretched, and then jumped down to stalk out of the room in search of a quieter place to nap.

"Well not only are you not going to miss the baking competition, I'm sure as heck not going to miss the craft fair. Yeah, it stinks that some poor young guy was assaulted. But we didn't hurt him, and I personally don't think that he would want us to miss the Christmas festivities on his behalf."

Incredulously, Mary looked at her friend. "I think that has to be the most amazing rationalization I've heard in a long time."

"Well, it's my rationalization, and I'm sticking to it. Yesterday was a pretty hellish day. But I am not letting one bad day ruin my holiday season."

Mary turned away to grab the coffee pot, then moved back to refill Sharon's cup and topped off her own. As she put the pot back onto the burner, she looked at the potentially winning pumpkin bread she had ready to go. It was beautifully wrapped in wax paper and topped with a cloth ribbon bow imprinted with holly.

She did believe this bread had a good chance of winning. And she did know that her Aunt Bridget would be ecstatic if Mary won with her recipe. But it felt weird to just go on with her life when someone nearly died last night and she didn't even know why.

She looked down at the bracelet on her right wrist. The silver Celtic knot glinted in the morning sunlight.

"Is missing the baking competition going to make that poor man any better, Miss Sassypants?" Mary heard her aunt's voice as clear as day in her head.

It was evident why Aunt Bridget and Sharon had been best friends. They both knew how to justify the things they wanted.

"Okay," Mary agreed with a sigh. "We'll go to the craft fair, and I will stay in the baking competition. But I'm also going to see if that pickpocket shows up there."

Mary couldn't stop thinking that the assaulted man found at the Peabody Mansion and the pickpocket were somehow related.

She couldn't pinpoint why that thought kept returning to her, but she had to follow her gut. The charm on her bracelet twinkled brightly, once again.

The Christmas craft fair and baking competition was one of the events that didn't take place in Edgartown. It took place in West Tisbury at the Grange Hall. Several heated tents had also been erected outside the Grange and lined with local artisans selling their crafts.

Crowds of shoppers already swarmed the grounds, perusing all the goodies from handmade Christmas decorations to quilts to hand-painted golf tees.

"I'm going to go drop off my bread to the judges, then I'm coming back to get some of these," Mary told Sharon, pointing to the golf tees painted with designs and other small images. "They'll be great for my dad's Christmas stocking."

"They will be," Sharon agreed.

"Do you want to come with me?" Mary asked, feeling a little uneasy despite the good cheer of the other shoppers.

"Nah, I'm going to browse around."

"Okay," not liking this plan at all, Mary added, "Just be careful."

Sharon chuckled. "What are the chances of getting pickpocketed twice?"

"I don't think it's like lightning strikes," Mary countered.

"I'll be careful," Sharon assured her as a vendor with sea glass earrings caught her attention.

Mary shook her head as her friend hurried away to inspect the jewelry more closely. She wished she could have her friend's cavalier attitude, but she had a feeling the pickpocket could be here today.

Mary decided the best thing to do was to drop off her pumpkin bread, and then return to Sharon.

She stepped out of the heated tent and headed toward the Grange building. The historic hall was just as busy inside as the outside. More vendors lined the interior wall inside the building, and at the back of the large hall the baking competition was set up with tables already laden with baked goods.

As she went to find Betty Marshall, the baking competition organizer, Mary sized up her competition. There were platters of cookies and beautifully decorated pies. And then she saw an impressive and towering croquembouche. The perfect pyramid of puff pastries glistened with golden glaze.

Darn, it was beautiful. And she had no doubt whose creation it was. Angela Jordan's.

Mary knew it was going to be hard for an easy bread recipe to compete with that. But it wasn't just the visuals, it had to taste good, too.

"Oh, good. you're here," Betty greeted Mary with a warm smile. "We are going to start the judging in about half an hour."

Mary hadn't realized she had been cutting it so close.

"You can set up your dish right there." Betty pointed to an open spot on the other side of the croquembouche.

Mary had a sneaking suspicion that nobody wanted their entries that close to that gorgeous display.

Oh well, may the best baker win.

Mary arranged her pumpkin bread on her Aunt Bridget's serving platter, a family heirloom painted with delicate holly leaves, and fine gold detailing. She hoped her aunt's platter would give her some added good luck.

She peeled back the wax paper, making the bread look like a present being opened on Christmas morning.

Mary stood back to study her presentation. It looked pretty. Simple yet elegant. She avoided comparing it to the impressive dessert next to hers.

As she walked down the length of the table to admire all of the other bakers' handiwork, Mary felt a chill steal over her. She paused and looked around the crowded room. Someone was watching her. She could feel their eyes like a brush against her skin.

Mary's scanning gaze stopped on a young girl. It was hard to tell how old she was from her waiflike appearance. Maybe ten or twelve.

As soon as the young girl realized that Mary had spotted her, she scurried away into the crowd. But something about the young girl seemed familiar. Mary got the definite feeling that she had seen the girl before, although she couldn't place where it could have been.

"Are you all ready for the big competition?"

Mary turned to see Nathan. Today, he wore a cream-colored fisherman sweater and his usual jeans. He looked as if he could be a model for some outdoorsy clothing magazine.

She managed a weak smile. "It looks like there's some stiff competition this year. But I'm glad you're here for moral support."

"I wouldn't miss it," he said. "I have to be here to see you take home the win."

Mary's face flushed with a happy warmth. But even as she was distracted by Nathan, she still had that strange, unsettling feeling of being watched.

"Well, I don't think I can just stand around here, waiting. It's making me nervous," Mary told him. "Sharon is out in the tents, probably buying one of everything. Would you like to go with me to find her?"

"Absolutely." He extended a hand for her to lead the way.

Mary headed back to the tent where the vendor was selling the golf tees. Sharon was still in the same tent although now she was carrying several bags. Mary's suspicion was validated. Sharon did love to shop.

"It looks like you've been finding some good things while I was away," Mary teased as she joined her friend.

Sharon smiled widely when she saw Nathan beside Mary. "It looks like you found a good thing, too."

If Nathan found Sharon's comment awkward, he didn't show any signs of it.

"How are you feeling today, Sharon?" he asked with an easy smile.

"I feel fine," Sharon assured him. "Although I suppose after the baking competition is over, I should probably head back to Peabody Mansion. The locksmith is coming this afternoon, and I'm not sure that I can trust the Sullivan brothers to handle things."

Mary was glad to see that Sharon was finally realizing that maybe Doug and Kevin were not the most reliable watchmen. She glanced around her, that odd being-watched feeling was creeping back.

She spotted the girl again; but this time, the young girl, whose complexion looked deathly pale against her black sweatshirt, was not watching her. The girl's gaze was locked on Sharon.

"Are you okay?" Nathan asked, seeing the wary puzzled expression on Mary's face.

Mary debated whether she should say anything. But finally, she looked back to her friends and said, "Do you see that girl over there?"

Without looking at the girl she tried to gesture subtly with just the slight jerk of her head. Both Nathan and Sharon glanced in the direction she indicated. "The little girl in a red Christmas dress?" Sharon asked.

"No," Mary replied, looking back toward where the girl in black had been standing. But she was no longer there.

Mary pulled a lock of her hair behind one ear and laughed slightly at her own silly nerves. "I thought I saw some girl who seemed to be following us. But now she's not there." She glanced around again. "I'm sure it was nothing. Just residual nerves from everything that's happened over the past couple days."

Sharon made a face in agreement. "I know we're all so rattled."

Mary nodded, deciding she was just reading too much into everything.

"And you're probably a little anxious about the baking competition, too" Nathan added.

"Speaking of which, I should probably pick up the few things I wanted to get and head back into the grange hall."

"Yes," Sharon encouraged "We don't want to miss seeing you kick some butt."

"You have to be kidding," Sharon muttered as they stood watching the judges. "All three of them?"

Mary's stomach sank when she saw that all three of the Gossip Gang were on the panel of judges for the baking competition. Thankfully, the entries didn't have any names attached to them. And maybe they hadn't seen Mary set out her bread.

"I can't believe Yvonne Luce has recovered enough to be here." Somehow Nathan somehow knew who Sharon was referring to. "I thought she was going to be hospitalized after last night."

Yvonne had sat in the ambulance outside Sharon's mansion last night wailing in hysteria and stopping only long enough to make sure that passersby had seen her dramatic display.

"There's no way she's going to miss a chance to judge others. After all, that's what the woman lives for," Sharon said with a scowl.

"Yes, it must get frustrating to be judgy without getting the appreciation she thinks she deserves," Mary said, watching closely as the three women moved to her pumpkin bread.

They each took a sample. Mary studied their expressions closely. All three of them looked less than impressed--although they had worn those same sour expressions at every entry thus far.

"It helps that there are seven judges, though," Mary continued, mostly to reassure herself. She still had a fighting chance even if the Gossip Gang snubbed her entry.

She continued to watch as they tasted the bread. To Mary's surprise, Gail and Winnie looked pleasantly surprised. Yvonne, though, pursed her lips as though she had been forced to eat moldy Wonder Bread.

Then the three women stopped in front of the croquembouche. This was the first time the Gossip Gang had looked truly impressed. And Mary couldn't even begrudge their reaction. The towering dessert was stunning.

They carefully took pieces of the caramelized pate a choux.

Mary's hopes sank as they savored each bite, talking excitedly about the pastry. Well, she suspected this still was not going to be her year.

Was it wrong that she just hoped the beautiful dessert wasn't Angela's? Yes, it was. This was just a friendly competition, and Mary wasn't going to allow herself to be petty like the Gossip Gang.

The judges had tasted all the baked goods, and now it was time to wait while they compared notes.

Betty finally approached the microphone set up next to the entry table.

"First of all, I want to applaud everyone who entered our contest. This group of bakers did not make it easy for us to come to a decision. But we do have this year's Christmas baking competition runner-up and winner."

Sharon patted Mary's arm reassuringly. And to Mary's other surprise, Nathan actually took her hand, squeezing it encouragingly.

Mary was so surprised by his unexpected touch that she nearly missed the announcement of the runner-up.

"This year's runner-up is Angela Jordan with her stunning croquembouche."

Mary blinked. She had known that had to have been Angela's entry. But she was only the runner-up?

"And this year's winner is Mary Hogan with her absolutely delicious holiday pumpkin bread!"

On either side of her Sharon and Nathan cheered loudly. Mary hated to admit it even to herself because she considered herself too grounded to feel quite so euphoric about a local baking competition, but she did feel like an actress going up to accept her Academy Award.

Except, of course, she wasn't actually going to go up and get her award. One of the local artisans still had to paint her name on the Christmas ornament. But she did smile and bow slightly.

"Congratulations," Angela said sincerely, being the very first one to congratulate her.

Mary immediately felt a little bit guilty for having such an intense competition with this woman. Angela was, in fact, a very nice lady.

"Thank you," Mary said. "Your croquembouche is truly gorgeous."

Angela smiled, clearly pleased with the compliment. "I had a lot of fun making it."

Mary nodded, realizing that was truly the point of this competition. She had let her competitive nature get the better of her. Although she'd be lying if she didn't say she was pretty darn excited to hang that ornament on her tree.

"Angela!" Yvonne called loudly.

Mary tried to make her escape before the ringleader of the Gossip Gang reached them, but Yvonne had clearly recovered from her distress of the previous night because she was over there in a shot.

"Angela, I just want you to know that I voted for your gorgeous dessert."

From the expression on her face, Angela clearly found Yvonne's loud comment awkward.

"Thank you, Yvonne," she managed, albeit smiling stiffly.

Yvonne lifted a paper plate to show that she had taken another serving of the croquembouche. "This is the quality of baking that should be winning awards."

Mary knew the comment was most definitely a jab at her entry.

As if to make a point, Yvonne took a relishing bite of the pate a choux puff pastry. Mary heard a loud crunch, although it didn't sound exactly like just the crackle of the caramelized sugar.

Immediately Yvonne's eyes widened, and her hand flew to her mouth. "I just cracked my tooth."

Standing by Mary, Sharon doubled over in laughter. Angela, on the other hand, looked totally dismayed.

Both Mary and Sharon saw Angela's worried expression. No doubt they knew that Yvonne would probably threaten to sue her—that was a typical Yvonne move. So, Sharon quickly added, "Don't worry, Angela, I'll gladly pay to get that tooth fixed for her."

CHAPTER 10

"Aren't you happy you didn't miss this? This was, by far, the best Christmas craft fair I have been to in—well, ever. Maybe the best craft fair of all time." Sharon said as they headed to the parking lot.

Sharon's delight in Yvonne's moment of instant karma hadn't waned.

Mary couldn't stop the smile returning to her own face. It was so rare that nasty people like Yvonne got their comeuppance. Yet, Yvonne Luce had gotten it two days in a row.

Although Mary hoped it wasn't at the expense of that poor guy in the hospital, or Angela's wallet. Although Mary had no doubt that Sharon would gladly pay to have Yvonne's cracked tooth fixed. If Yvonne could tell everyone about the injured guy in Sharon's bathroom, it only seemed fair that Sharon could tell everyone about having to pay to fix Yvonne's tooth to spare Angela a potential lawsuit.

The two of them reached Sharon's car. Nathan had to leave because he had a big shipment of cheese to deliver to the Harborside Inn in Edgartown. It seemed he had sneaked in a quick trip to the craft fair just to be here for the baking competition. Mary tried very hard not to get moony over the thought, but as usual, she knew she was probably grinning like a fool.

Today, had definitely been an improvement over the events of yesterday. Well, except for the date. Her date with Nathan had saved yesterday from being a total wash.

As Mary reflected happily on her win, which was still drying in the bag looped over her left arm. suddenly a movement caught her attention amid the rows of parked cars.

It was the girl. She stood watching her over the flatbed of a beat-up, green truck. But now she wasn't alone. Beside her stood a taller figure in a gray hoodie. When the two of them realized Mary had noticed them, they ran off quickly, disappearing among the people and parked vehicles.

Who were they? And why did something about the way they raced away seem oddly familiar?

Sharon interrupted her pondering. "Do you want me to drop you off at your place? Or did you want to come to the mansion with me?"

Mary's gut instincts told her that she should go to the mansion. But she didn't say that to her friend. Sharon would just start asking a bunch of questions that she didn't have any answers to, not yet anyway.

"I'll go with you. I don't like the idea of you being there by yourself."

"I won't be there by myself. The Sullivan brothers are still there."

After they settled into Sharon's BMW, Mary gave her a dubious look.

Acknowledging the look, Sharon held both palms up in the air. "I know, I know. If I ever need someone to guard my place for me again, believe me, it won't be the Sullivan brothers."

That was reassuring, at least. Mary studied the parking lot as they left, hoping she could get another glimpse of those two kids. Although what would really be reassuring to know was who they were and what they wanted?

When they got to the Peabody Mansion, Mary was pleased to see the locksmith's van parked out front. That was a good sign. And an even better sign was to find both Doug and Kevin awake and greeting them as they came to the door.

"Nick just got here about twenty minutes ago," Doug informed Sharon.

Mary assumed that Nick was the locksmith.

"That's great!" Sharon seemed clearly as happy as Mary to see that the Sullivan brothers were now realizing that they needed to be a bit more on their game.

While Sharon went to find Nick to talk to him about the new locks and how they worked with the security system, Mary decided to make some coffee. And maybe admire her "major award," as the father from A Christmas Story would say.

But as she moved around the kitchen, filling the coffee pot and looking for a cup, her brain started to hum loudly.

Her first instinct was to ignore it. Old habits died hard. But then she looked down at her bracelet. Maybe she really did need to try to embrace her abilities.

Because caffeine was just as important as self-acceptance, she finished preparing the coffee pot. Then she sat down on one of the barstools at the island, closed her eyes, and just tried to let her thoughts relax.

She needed to go outside. This realization came to her, so strongly and clearly, it could've been an actual person telling her what she had to do.

She went to the back door and unlocked it. It didn't look as if Nick had changed out this lock. And as she touched the deadbolt Mary got a clear image of that young man who had been assaulted. He had staggered into the house, through the back door. But when he heard people moving around inside the mansion, he'd made it into the bathroom to hide but collapsed before he could lock the door behind him.

He had used Sharon's keys. Did that mean he was the pickpocket? She was sure it must mean that, how else would he have the mansion keys?

As powerful as it was, she realized this vision wasn't why her psychic ability was telling her to go outside. She still had that feeling that she physically had to go out to the backyard.

When she stepped outside, she wasn't sure, though, what she should be looking for. She studied the ground, but it was now impossible to tell if the man's footprints were out there or not. The bright sun from earlier in the day had melted much of the light snowfall from the evening before. The ground was just patches of snow and brown grass.

She was sure if there had been any trail leading from somewhere else to the back door then, Tom or Sheriff Wilks would have seen it last night.

So, what was she out here to find? She wandered aimlessly, trying to empty her mind. She looked over at the Vanderhoop house.

Everything seemed to be quiet over there today. Even the windows were dark, and she wondered if the nephew and family had decided to leave. Or clear out because of all the police presence last night.

Mary still didn't believe that the man was supposed to be over there. And she didn't think it took any psychic abilities to figure that out. Although maybe it did. Heaven knew, the Edgartown police didn't seem to get the same vibe that she and Sharon had gotten.

As she stared at the now dark house she noticed something. A glint of sunlight on something metal. Right near the bulkhead.

Just to be sure she didn't see any movement inside Mary stared at the house. The house looked deserted, but she wasn't sure she could trust that. That creep might be right inside one of the windows, watching, and she wouldn't be able to see him in the shadows. But she suddenly knew that whatever that thing lying beside the cellar door was exactly what she was supposed to be out here to find.

She geared herself up, then rushed over to grab the item. Without looking back at the Vanderhoop house she strode quickly back to Sharon's door. Once back inside the kitchen with the door locked behind her, she looked at the cold metal item that she held clutched in her hand.

It was a watch.

A very old pocket watch to be exact. The face cover was embossed with a seascape: a lighthouse with a rocky shore and a small sailing ship.

She flipped the antique over and saw the initials H.W. engraved on the back.

Suddenly, an image of the well-known Martha's Vineyard author Georgia Williams appeared in her mind. This pocket watch belonged to her. Mary was sure of it.

Before she even fully realized what she was planning to do, she scurried through the mansion looking for Sharon. Her friend was at a door that led out to a side porch from the library. Sharon was talking to Nick, the locksmith, when Mary rushed into the room.

"Mary, is everything all right?" Sharon asked. From Sharon's somewhat scared tone, Mary realized she must have looked a bit shaken, so, she managed a calm smile.

"Yes, I was just wondering if I could borrow your car for a minute. I realize there's something I forgot to do."

She could tell from Sharon's puzzled expression that her friend wanted to question her further, but she simply nodded.

"Of course, I'm going to be here for a while. My keys are in my purse by the front door."

Mary thanked her and hurried out of the mansion.

Mary only had a vague idea where on the island Georgia Williams lived. She knew that it was over in Menemsha, an old fishing village on Martha's Vineyard that had become popular with artisans and other creative individuals. Which was why the information had stuck in Mary's head. She thought that was the perfect place for a writer to live and write.

She drove to that side of the island, only stopping at a gas station that looked as if it had probably been in operation since the '50s. When she stepped out into the station, which also served as a general store, she noticed a craggy old man in a greasy baseball cap standing behind the register in front of a wall lined with cigarettes and cigars.

This man didn't appear to be the kind of guy who would be interested in Georgia Williams' books, but he did look like someone who had been on the island for a long time.

"Hi, I'm looking for where Georgia Williams lives," she said, with a polite smile.

The man's gray-green eyes, which reminded Mary of the ocean waves, assessed her for a moment. "She doesn't like visitors."

"Oh, she knows I'm coming."

"Well, if she knows you're coming, why didn't you ask her where she lives?"

He had a valid point there. Mary decided to just go for the truth, wondering why she hadn't opted for that in the first place.

She reached into her coat pocket and pulled out the pocket watch. "Okay, I'm actually trying to find her house to return this to her. I'm pretty certain it's something she lost."

The man studied her for a moment longer, barely glancing at the pocket watch in her hand.

"She lives on the third road up on your right." He nodded his head in the direction she should take. "All the way at the end."

Mary thanked the man and hurried back out to Sharon's car. It didn't take too long to find the road he was talking about. Or at least she hoped it was the right one since this road was narrow and unpaved. But she followed it to the end. Nestled in some trees right on the very coastline of the island, stood a quaint, picturesque cottage.

As she got out of the car, she could hear the waves crashing against the rocky shoreline. While the house itself was small and unpretentious, she could well understand why Ms. Williams would want to be in this location. It was stunning!

She opened the small picket fence that surrounded what Mary imagined was an impressive rock and flower garden in the summer.

From inside the house, she heard the sharp yips of several dogs. With her four-legged security system, Ms. Williams peered through the window of her front door. The older woman frowned slightly but then shooed her dogs back as she stepped out onto her small front porch.

"Can I help you?" she asked her tone curious but a little aloof.

Mary smiled. "I'm very sorry to just show up at your house like this. But I believe I found something today that might belong to you."

The older woman tilted her head slightly. "Belongs to me?"

Mary dug in her pocket and retrieved the watch. She stepped forward to show her the piece in her open palm.

Without hesitation, Ms. Williams stepped down the two steps to take it.

She stared at the watch for a moment, then looked up, her cool gaze replaced by one of gratitude. "Where did you find this?"

"I found it on the lawn of a neighbor's house." Mary decided it was easier not to get into the specifics of it, especially since it was Sharon's house.

"On a neighbor's lawn? Really? I thought I had lost it."

"On the night of the Edgartown lighthouse lighting?"

The older woman blinked at her. "Yes, how did you know?"

"Did you notice anything strange that night? Maybe somebody bumped into you? Or they were hanging around, standing too close?"

Ms. Williams considered that. "Well, I'm not a huge fan of crowds, but I sort of felt like everyone was standing too close." The woman smiled slightly. "But now that you mention it, I do remember there was this person in a black hooded sweatshirt that was lingering around the stage area. I do remember thinking that was odd. Do you think that person had something to do with the watch?"

Mary paused to consider her statement. A person in a black-hooded sweatshirt. That wasn't the same person she had seen at the lighting ceremony. The person she had seen stumbling around was in a gray sweatshirt. She was sure of it.

"I was just curious if you saw anyone because there has been an issue with pickpocketing on the island," Mary explained.

"Pickpocketing?" The older woman was clearly surprised, but after a moment or so she started to grin. "That is very Dickensian for the holiday season."

Mary held back a full laugh. "Yes, I suppose it is."

"Well, I'm not sure if I just dropped it and someone else found it, or if it was stolen, but I can't tell you how pleased I am to get it back. It was my father's, and I guess I'm a bit superstitious, but I've always kept it with me, as sort of a good luck charm."

Mary thought of the bracelet on her wrist. "I think it's important to have good luck charms. Especially when they remind us of someone we loved."

Ms. Williams curled her fingers tighter around the watch absently holding it to her chest. "I am just so glad to have it back. Thank you."

"You're so welcome," Mary replied as she turned to go back out the gate.

The older woman called after her suddenly. "What is your name?"

Mary turned back to her. "Mary Hogan."

"Mary Hogan, how did you know this belonged to me?"

Mary hesitated, not sure how to explain. Or if she wanted to.

Georgia Williams must have seen the indecision on Mary's face because she simply shrugged and answered for her. "A bit of Christmas magic, I guess."

Mary gave Ms. Williams an appreciative smile "Yes, I guess so."

As she waved her goodbyes she heard a symphony of yaps greeting Georgia Williams as she entered back into her house.

But once back in Sharon's car, Mary frowned. She was certainly glad that Ms. Williams had got her father's watch back, but she hadn't gotten much information from her. At least nothing that seemed particularly useful.

So why did her abilities have her find that watch? Maybe just to make sure it was returned to someone who was heartbroken to have lost it?

She turned the car around and headed back out the dirt road. The only piece of information that Mary found interesting was that Ms. Williams had noted somebody in a black hoodie had been lingering around. Not a gray hoodie.

Then Mary heard Georgia Williams' voice in her head, "That's very Dickensian."

"Dickensian," she said aloud to herself. "Yes, maybe it is all more Dickensian than we realized."

CHAPTER 11

"Did you get everything done you needed to?" Sharon asked when Mary returned to the Peabody Mansion.

"Yes, I think I did. But do you mind if I go into your basement?"

Sharon gave her a curious look. The way she was acting, Sharon wondered what Mary was up to. But Sharon managed to say, "Sure, that's not a problem. Do you want me to go down with you?"

Mary shook her head. "I just want to check something out that Nathan mentioned when he and Doug were looking around the house the night of the tour."

"Definitely, take a look. I'm sure you'll fill me in when you're ready." Sharon felt very curious but didn't want to intrude.

Mary smiled. "You know I will."

Sharon had been her sounding board for all her crazy sleuthing ideas. And Mary was truly happy to share anything with her that she could.

Mary found the doorway to the basement in the back hallway. She was glad she didn't have to go outside and struggle with a bulkhead like next door.

The basement of the Peabody Mansion was truly just a cellar with dirt floors and stone walls. There wasn't much down there since it wasn't a particularly clean or dry place to use as storage. Mary was glad. The open space made it feel a little less creepy. But she stayed focused on the one thing that had attracted her interest: the small window that Nathan said had been open. There were actually a few small rectangular windows built into the rock walls. But it didn't matter which one had been open, Mary just needed to see the size of them.

Nathan was right, they were too small for an average-sized adult to get through them. But it might be possible for a thin girl to fit through them. In fact, she felt pretty confident that one could.

She headed back upstairs to get her cell phone out of her purse. She needed to call Tom.

As was customary for her friend, Tom answered after the first ring. "Constable Andrews."

"I think I figured out what's going on around here," Mary said without any preamble.

"Okay," Tom replied without further questioning. "I'm just finishing up at the station, I'll be over in about half an hour."

"I'm at the Peabody Mansion." Mary hung up her phone. She went to the dining room and looked over at the house next door. There was a light on at the back of the house. Good, they hadn't left yet.

Tom was there within twenty minutes, anxious to hear Mary's theory. The locksmith had finished, and Sharon had sent Doug and Kevin home. Now the three friends sat in the kitchen with cups of coffee as Mary started to explain her theory.

"I was out in this backyard today and I discovered a pocket watch. When I picked it up, I just knew that it belonged to Georgia Williams.

So, I went to her house to return it, hoping that maybe she knew something about the person who stole it. Maybe she saw something or heard something. I don't know."

"And did she?" Tom asked.

Mary shook her head. "No. The only thing she could tell me was that she noticed a person in a black hooded sweatshirt sort of hanging around. Which didn't make sense to me because I saw someone at the lighting ceremony that I thought was acting strangely, too. But the person I saw was in a gray hooded sweatshirt."

"Well, like I told you, eyewitnesses notoriously get details wrong. Not to mention, it was already dark out," Tom said.

"That's true. But Ms. Williams did say something else that got me thinking. She said that pickpockets were very Dickensian," Mary told them.

"She's got a point," Sharon said, taking a sip of the martini she just made. "I guess in Martha's Vineyard even the crimes are quaint."

Mary wasn't sure that quaint was the right word for what was going on. Or at least, what she thought was going on.

"And it occurred to me that maybe there was more than one pickpocket."

"That does make sense," Tom agreed, with a nod. "Sheriff Wilks did mention that a lot of people have been hit."

"And given that I found the pocket watch on the Vanderhoop property I think it's also safe to assume that whoever is staying over there might be a part of this pickpocketing ring, if you will."

"That's a good supposition, Mary." Tom looked thoughtfully at his friend. "That does seem to be a bit more than a coincidence."

"Then I started thinking more about this whole Dickens analogy. Wasn't it true that in Oliver Twist there was one guy who had a whole ring of pickpockets?" Mary asked.

Sharon chimed in, "Yes, Fagin. I remember him from the musical Oliver! in Boston… Oh let's see, maybe three years ago."

"So you think that the guy next-door is sending out others to do his dirty work for him?" Tom asked.

"Yes, maybe. Didn't the sheriff say he was there with his kids?" Mary pointed out.

Tom replied "Yes, he did. I have that fact written in my notes."

"But how does the young guy beaten to a pulp in my bathroom tie in?" Sharon asked, frowning in confusion. "Does he tie in?"

Mary answered, "My guess is maybe he didn't want to do these criminal jobs. I think he came over here, pretending to be a cop, to try to warn us without tipping off his father, or whoever that guy is."

"But 'the nephew' still tried to break in," Sharon said, not following the logic.

"I think that the older guy did send him over here to find out about our plans. Like whether we would be staying in the mansion over the holidays. And maybe to find out if this place had an alarm system. Which means our fake police officer didn't tell him that you had an alarm.

Maybe he wanted the alarm to go off so the ringleader would get caught," Mary deduced.

Sharon pondered that. "And then 'the nephew' beat the ever-living daylights out of the kid for screwing up." She took a sip of her martini, then widened her eyes in amazement. "If you're right, this is a pretty incredible plan."

Tom took a sip of his coffee, then set it aside. "I definitely think it's worth going over there to have a talk with him."

Mary put down her coffee, too. "I'm going with you."

"I don't think that that's a good idea. We already know this guy has the potential for extreme violence," Tom continued as he stood.

"I don't think it's a good idea for you to go over there either," Sharon added, grimacing at their law enforcement friend. "Don't you think you should contact Sheriff Wilks and get back up?"

"Not quite yet. I don't want to have police cruisers showing up here and tipping this guy off that we know something. I just want to feel him out."

"I'm going," Mary insisted. "If I'm right, there's at least two kids over there, and I think we should get them out before you talk to that guy."

Tom considered her point. "Okay, but you need to figure out how to get the kids out, before I talk to him."

Mary nodded. She was nervous, but she kept thinking of that girl at the craft fair. Her pale, serious face. She needed help. And Mary had no doubt that she was over there in the Vanderhoop mansion.

Mary's whole body prickled with apprehension. The extreme humming in her head didn't help. But she also knew it was telling her she was on the right track.

Tom knocked on the Vanderhoop's front door. There was no answer. He waited a moment, and then knocked again, louder this time.

Still nothing.

"Maybe they're not here," he voiced quietly.

"No, they're here. I can sense it."

Tom rapped on the door again. This time they could hear hushed voices from inside. Although they couldn't make out any words, they could tell from the insistent tones, that whoever was in there was arguing just above a whisper.

Then, to Mary's surprise, the door opened a crack. A dark eye, and half of a narrow, pale face, peeked out at them.

It was the girl from the craft fair.

"Hi there," Tom said warmly. "Is your father home?"

To both of their surprise the door opened more, and a taller young boy appeared behind the girl. Mary recognized him as the one who the older guy had been yelling at as he'd left the house and run down the street.

"He's not here," the boy muttered, his tone cold, and his dark eyes much like the younger girl's, wary.

"Well, that's okay," Mary chimed in. "We were just stopping by to see if you wanted to come over for some cookies and hot chocolate. We have a lot left over from the tour last night. I'm not sure if you were around but we had an accident over at the house and had to call the tour off early."

She watched the kids' reactions carefully. If they knew of the young man who had been in Sharon's bathroom, they'd react.

Sure enough, the two kids exchanged a look. The girl stared at the older boy almost pleadingly, but the boy tried to remain stoic.

Before the boy could say anything, though, the girl stepped out onto the porch with Mary and Tom.

"That would be nice," she said, smiling, although Mary could still see the uncertainty in her dark eyes.

This girl wanted to trust them. Mary knew she needed help, and she was going to see that the young girl got it.

The boy looked as if he wanted to argue, but again, the girl spoke first. "Come on, Ben, I think cookies and hot chocolate sound good."

Reluctantly, silently, the boy followed them outside.

If Sharon was surprised to see Mary and Tom return with two children, she didn't show it. Instead, she bustled around to get them some cookies.

"Darn, it looks as if I am out of hot chocolate," she said with a regretful smile. "But I do have milk. Is that okay?"

Almost at the same time both kids looked down, then back up again and nodded "Ok". Mary got the feeling they really were like the pickpockets in Oliver Twist, sad little waifs who were half-starved.

After they were settled at the kitchen island with cookies and tall glasses of cold milk, Mary and Tom exchanged a look and watched them eat. Mary knew that each of them wanted to start asking these kids questions, but they had to handle it carefully. They didn't want to distress the children any more than they clearly already were. And they didn't want to scare them away.

To Mary's surprise, it was Sharon who made the comment to get the conversation started.

"Oh," she said, her tone casual. "I got a call while you were next door. It was the hospital. They wanted to update me on the poor young man who was here last night."

Both children stopped eating to listen.

"Such a terrible thing for him to be hurt so badly," Sharon continued, shaking her head and covertly glancing at the kids.

The two children exchanged looks. Mary could see the worry on both their faces. Sharon's prompt worked. This time, it was the boy who spoke first.

"Is--is he going to be okay?"

"I think so," Sharon reassured him.

The boy and girl looked at each other again, and Mary could witness the relief on their faces. She knew Sharon hadn't actually talked to anyone at the hospital, so she hoped that the claim would prove to be true. Clearly, these kids were very concerned about that young man.

"Do you know him?" Mary asked gently.

"He's our brother," the girl answered without hesitation.

"Shut up, Sarah," Ben warned.

But Sarah had clearly had enough of whatever they had been going through, and she was done staying silent. She met Mary's gaze, and Mary had immediate compassion for the girl's desperate need to be able to trust her. To trust all of them.

"Our dad did that to him."

Mary's stomach turned at the thought. These poor children! "Why?"

Ben seemed to realize that now that Sarah had started talking, they had no choice but to hope that these three adults would help them.

"Jack, that is our brother, told our dad that he was going to go to the police," Ben softly attempted to explain.

"Our dad was making us steal things," Sarah admitted, her small voice ashamed. "He threatened us if we didn't."

"Did he make you come into this house?" Mary asked, keeping her tone gentle and without judgment.

"At first he just made us a list of stuff to steal off people. But then he decided there were plenty of rich people on this island that left their houses empty for the winter."

"And that's when he started having Sarah go into the houses," Ben interjected. "She's small enough to get into a lot of places. And Jack told him that was enough. That he couldn't do that to Sarah anymore because she's only twelve."

"And our dad started hitting Jack," Sarah said, as her dark eyes filled with tears.

Mary wanted to cry with these kids. What father could do this to his own children? Mary moved to hug the girl. She was surprised at how readily the child accepted her affection.

"We're going to get you help," Mary assured her.

"Will you call our mom?" the girl asked her, looking painfully hopeful. So, these kids did have a mother somewhere.

"Yes, absolutely," Mary assured her.

Mary looked at Tom as she still held the girl. He seemed as distressed as Mary felt. He got up from his chair and headed for the front door, and Mary suspected he was leaving to call Sheriff Wilks.

Everything moved quickly after that. The man next door was arrested without incident when he returned to the Vanderhoop residence. It turned out he was really a 'Mark Sykes' from New York—no relation to the Vanderhoops, as expected. He'd done some odd jobs for them at their main estate in Westchester County, NY. That was where he formulated the plan to empty out their mansion in Martha's Vineyard. It had been easy enough for him to figure out exactly where their place was on the island, and then steal a set of keys.

Mark was also in the middle of a bitter custody battle with his ex-wife. So, he took the kids and disappeared to Martha's Vineyard. Once he saw the wealth of Edgartown, though, he decided he could use the kids to rob more than just the Vanderhoop place. Mark had seen the Island as the perfect spot to make a fortune, and then disappear to somewhere else with his children. But Jack had decided he wasn't going to let their father do this. They hadn't dared to contact their mother, however, because Mark had threatened to kill her if they did. And they believed he was violent enough to do it.

Mary did call the hospital and learned that Jack would fortunately be okay. He had regained consciousness and was already telling the hospital staff about what his father was doing.

Mary had asked the police if she could keep Sarah and Ben with her until their mother was contacted, but Sheriff Wilks told her that she would have to let Social Services handle the children.

Thankfully, Mary knew the head of Social Services on the Island, having catered her daughter's wedding last summer. So, Mary was able to talk to Jill Sanders and get some reassurance that Ben and Sarah would be safe and properly protected until their mother was located.

Jill even promised to let the younger kids go see their brother in the hospital.

"Everything will be fine," Tom assured Mary as they watched the kids leave with Jill. "If you hadn't put those pieces together, things could've gotten a lot worse for those kids."

"I don't understand why Sykes just didn't leave after we found Jack," Sharon wondered out loud.

"Pure greed," Tom said as he turned to face Sharon more directly. "That basement at the Vanderhoops is just loaded with stolen goods. But Sykes couldn't figure out how to move all the stuff out of there with the police around your place. Jack wisely took the opportunity to come over here. He got the help he needed. He also got the police right where his father couldn't get away with any of his loot."

"Are the kids going to be in any legal trouble?" Mary probed.

"No. All three of them are minors, and they were being forced by their father to do illegal acts. They will be fine, no legal trouble." Tom reassured her.

"Those poor kids," Sharon said, shaking her head and looking over at the Vanderhoop house. "What a horrible Christmas for them."

Mary sighed. "It was a horrible Christmas. But I think now that they'll be back with their mother, it might be the best Christmas of their lives."

CHAPTER 12

Mary's Emerald Inn was filled with family and friends and Christmas cheer. A fire crackled in the fireplace of her living room. The lights on her tree sparkled, the room was alive with the Christmas music of Nat King Cole, and the chatter and laughter of those she cared most about in the world. It all felt like Santa's cherished gift to her—Christmas unwrapped.

Her father and Tom sat in wingback chairs, having a glass of brandy, and discussing golf scores. Swaying and humming slightly to the music, Angelica Moonstone stood admiring the ornaments on Mary's tree, especially the Award-Winning one! Sharon, with her ever-present martini, was on the couch telling the Sykes children some tall tale about one of her childhood Christmases. Something terribly cliche like walking miles through the snow to get a Christmas tree.

The Sykes children actually looked like children now, their complexions rosier and their cheeks fuller. Well, except for poor Jack, who still sported bruises from standing up to his father. But even he looked happy.

Nancy, the children's mother, stepped out from the kitchen where she had been helping Mary with the Christmas dinner.

"I think the turkey is just about done," the petite brunette said. She had arrived in Martha's Vineyard as soon as she heard that her children had been located. Jack hadn't been able to travel due to his injuries, so Mary had insisted that Nancy, Sarah, Jack and Ben all stay at the inn.

Having them there had been wonderful, just adding to the joy and magic of the Christmas season.

Mary followed Nancy back into the kitchen to check the food.

"Wow!" Mary said, pleased as she took the golden turkey out of the oven. "This looks as if it's going to be perfect."

Nancy smiled at her. "You certainly have given me and my children a perfect Christmas. I can't thank you enough."

"You're so welcome," Mary said, returning the smile. "All of you have made my Christmas very special, too. And I'm just glad I could help."

There was a knock at the door. Mary left Nancy, who was checking the other side dishes and hurried to the door. Her last guest had arrived for dinner.

She opened the door to see Nathan wearing the ugliest sweater she had ever seen and laughed out loud in spite of herself! What she thought were supposed to be reindeer, although they looked more like blobs with antlers, pranced across his chest. They were surrounded by snowflakes in various bright colors, too. And there were even pom-poms sewn onto the knit material for good measure.

"You look, um, very dashing tonight." She grinned.

Nathan held out his hands to each side and curtsied in appreciation of her bad reindeer pun.

"I figured it wasn't really Christmas unless somebody showed up in an ugly sweater."

"I'm glad you decided to make that sacrifice."

He offered her a bottle of wine and then held something up over her head.

She glanced up to see what he was waving above them.

"I also figured it wasn't really Christmas unless we had one kiss under the mistletoe."

Mary stared at him, surprised. And thrilled. She held his gaze for a moment, smiling warmly, then closed her eyes and tilted her head back just a little. Then he leaned down to kiss her. For a while longer the celebration going on behind her was totally forgotten as she reveled in their kiss.

And what a kiss.

When they parted, Nathan smiled crookedly at her, looking ridiculously handsome, even in his ugly sweater. "Merry Christmas, Mary Hogan."

"Merry Christmas, Nathan Stewart."

Merry Christmas, everyone...

BONUS RECIPE

Aunt Bridget's Pumpkin Bread

Prep 15 min, Total 3 hr 25 min – baking & cooling, Servings 24

Fire up your coziest playlist, grab your baking gear, and get ready for Aunt Bridget's incredible homemade pumpkin bread. A pumpkin loaf makes for a great gift! The best part? With only 95 calories per serving (12 servings per loaf), this moist pumpkin bread won't completely derail your diet.

Ingredients

1 can (15-16 ounces) pumpkin (not pumpkin pie mix)

2 cups sugar (or comparable sugar substitute like Truvia - Not Stevia

it bakes bitter)

2/3 cup shortening (use either coconut oil or a light vegetable oil)

2 teaspoons vanilla

½ cup water

4 eggs

3 cups all-purpose white flour

2/3 cup coarsely chopped nuts- either walnuts or pecans

2/3 cup raisins, if desired

2 teaspoons baking soda

1/2 teaspoon baking powder

1 teaspoon salt

1 teaspoon ground cinnamon

1 teaspoon ground cloves

Steps:

1. Heat oven to 350°F. Grease bottoms only of 2 loaf pans, 9x5x3 or 8 1/2x4 1/2x2 1/2 inches, with your shortening. (Greasing just the bottom of your loaf pan and not the sides will help your Pumpkin Bread to form a loaf with gently rounded tops, without creating ridges along the edges.)
2. Stir together pumpkin, sugar, oil, vanilla and eggs and water into a large bowl. Stir in remaining ingredients. Pour into pans.
3. Bake 8-inch loaves for about 60 minutes, 9-inch loafs for about1 hour 10 minutes or until a toothpick inserted in center comes out clean. (Start checking with the toothpick test about 5 minutes before end of bake time, as oven temperatures can vary)
4. Cool for 10 minutes. Loosen sides of loaves from pans; remove from pans and place top side up on a wire rack. Cool completely, about 2 hours, before slicing. Wrap tightly and store at room temperature for up to 4 days, or refrigerate up to 10 days, or freeze for up to 6 months.

Tips from Aunt Bridget

- Leave the raisins out if you don't like them. This pumpkin nut bread still will be delicious!

- You can swap pieces of dried fruit (cranberries or cherries) or mini chocolate chips for the raisins. Try walnuts with dried cherries, yum! Just be sure to use the same amount of ingredients.

- Serve with Irish Coffee or Regular coffee if you must. Enjoy!

ABOUT THE AUTHOR

Rose Malone was born and raised in Massachusetts. She spent over 20 summers working and vacationing at Martha's Vineyard. Rose developed a lifelong love for this "Storybook Island" with its rich history and the amazing people who make it their seasonal or year-round home.

When she isn't writing, she is an intuitive psychotherapist known for her warmth, wit, and wisdom. Rose is married to the love of her life and lives in Southern California with their 2 German Shepherds and Maine Coon Cats who provide inspiration for her Martha's Vineyard Cozy Mysteries.

Other Martha's Vineyard cozy mystery books by Rose Malone

Perfect Plate of Poison, August 2023

Murder at the Emerald Inn, September 2023

You can contact Rose Malone directly at hello@rosemalonebooks.com or you can visit RoseMaloneBooks.com to get a complimentary copy of her first book Perfect Plate Of Poison, and to find out about upcoming books, events, and promos.

Made in the USA
Columbia, SC
07 December 2023